CLAIRE RUDY FOSTER

SHINE OF THE EVER

STEREO

*short stories*

interlude press • new york

ISBN 13: 978-1-945053-87-0 (trade)
ISBN 13: 978-1-945053-88-7 (ebook)
Published by Interlude Press
http://interludepress.com
BOOK AND COVER DESIGN BY CB Messer
10 9 8 7 6 5 4 3 2 1

interlude ✦ press • new york

*This one's for The Dude and Lewis Jones.*

# CONTENTS

# THE PIXIES

OUR PARENTS ALL THINK WE'RE weirdos. We're not good enough for them but we're good enough for each other. The music is too loud, and we are packed tighter than canned tuna, shoulder against shoulder. Heads moving more or less in rhythm, as if in agreement: Yes, we are the fuck-ups. Yes, we'll disappoint you. We did it wrong. We win at making better mistakes.

Some of us look like punks and some don't but we're all wearing the costume of belonging. We're not welcome in your church, you know. This club is our church and it's loud, loud, loud. The voice of God is in the bass reverb and the lyrics' rising incantation. You told us that we were as good as dead. You said we have that gay disease. You copy and steal from us; you never give credit. You're desperate to catch whatever we've got.

We congregate to forget how sick you make us.

We don't distinguish between wrong and right; we are what is real.

The singer has a voice like fighting tigers. She raises her microphone over the crowd of ecstatic faces, and we shout back to her. The sound pushes on the walls, ceiling, floor, growling into something massive and golden.

When we're together, we forget that we are hopeless.

We are something else and we are part of each other.

We will never fit. Why would we want to be like you? Go to school, get some debt and a silly job? We might even get married, now that it's legal. But what's the point of acting straight? We're no good at it anyway; you tell us all the time.

We will do things our way. We will stomp to the office in work boots and wear safety pins in our ears. We will leave the glitter in our eyebrows after Pride. We will grow old gracelessly and live in sin and teach our children to argue with anyone, even us, even God. *Even I'll adore you,* we sing, even as our hearts ball up in our throats.

If Darwin was right, we are better than you. *My Velouria.* The chorus comes and we are a mass of bliss and fury and love and pain and truth and sound.

*Finally through the roof.*

We are going to shake you loose.

# STAY COOL

MEN INVENTED RELIGION AS A means of getting their way. To Jessie, that was the only possible explanation for why she was moving out of Seth's house. She was on her own again.

She pulled Seth's truck into the parking lot of her new apartment complex, the last building with vacancies in a low-rent neighborhood in Portland, and began unloading and carrying boxes. Her crappy, two-bedroom shoebox of an apartment still had dings in its walls from the last tenant, a smoker with cats who stank up the carpets and closets. Jessie shifted the crate of inhalers, steam vaporizer parts, and nebulizer that she'd need to plug in before Neil stayed the night.

Neil had asthma that cleared while they were living with Seth. Now, it would probably come back. Seth's backyard was a field of lavender and soft lamb's ear and purple butterfly bush that attracted pollinators during the day and bats at night.

As Jessie went back down to get more boxes out of Seth's truck, she passed a mother in a burka with three children in tow. The mother went quiet as Jessie passed them on the stairs, then started up again once she'd reached the next landing.

Mothers said the same things in every language; theirs was a different kind of faith.

Jessie's boxes were dented and had been taped up many times. The heaviest one was books, the last things Jessie kept from her brief marriage to Neil's father. Four Bibles in various translations, a Quran, the poems of Khalil Gibran, an annotated *Wasteland* with Pound's handwriting in the margins.

Seth's text said, "Leave the keys on the seat when you park at my place."

She couldn't work out a response to that. The words fit together too tightly for her to get through. He'd lent her the truck and a thousand dollars for the apartment deposit: one boundary mortared on top of another. He'd made it so it was impossible to go back.

The prophet Muhammad said that marriage is a basis for blessings and children are an abundance of mercy. Every Muslim family in the apartment complex had at least two, one in a stroller and one tagging along when they walked to the nearby mosque.

The injunction to have more children was a hadith, said to come from Muhammad himself.

Neil's father found an abundance of commonalities between the sects. *Of course*, Jessie thought. He was fluent in God, and all religions were invented by men. They were the language of men—a way to explain to them why their wives did awful things, why their children got sick and died, why they weren't half the men their neighbors were—a language that ensured men could find acceptance somewhere, since they were incapable of accepting themselves.

Jessie went back to the truck. There were only a few things left, so she overloaded herself trying to make one less trip up the stairs. Her legs were already burning. She'd gotten weak again. When she was with Seth in the beginning, they ran together in the morning and did push-ups after in the cool grass of the park near his house. She could walk home beside him feeling fresh as a bride and new, with the sun coming up and her sweat turning chill as it soaked into her shirt. She always went into Seth's house the back way, up the driveway, so she could peek at Neil. It was a gift to find him sleeping peacefully in the back bedroom with the windows open so the lavender breeze could come in and touch his skin. Under the window, Seth installed a small, bubbling fountain, which made Neil's favorite noise. After years of sleeping with a CPAP machine strapped to his face, looking like a tiny Darth Vader, he was temporarily unhooked and breathing independently. The fountain masked the sound of Jessie's sneakers on the gravel path and the secret words she said to Seth when only God was listening.

And now she got winded just climbing the stairs. Jessie dodged a group of shrieking kids brandishing Nerf guns. Her arms were full of her son's toys and, unable to see over her load of brightly colored plush and plastic, she almost stepped on one boy who got too close. He racked his toy M-16 and darted back, a child soldier. *Do not compare this with the evening news.*

She walked up the three flights of stairs and deposited the bag of toys, then sat on the thin brown rug. The toys spilled out of the bag and tugged it sideways, down, down to the carpet, where its contents tumbled out. A stuffed lion stared at her with glassy yellow eyes.

She picked it up. Her son might be here Thursday, if the hospital released him from this last stay in the oxygen tent. She had a day to make the apartment nice and put his bedroom together. And figure out a story about why Seth wasn't around anymore, just like his father, and why they were better off this way: always, better off alone.

JESSIE FELL ASLEEP JUST AFTER sunset. She meant to do more, but inflating two air mattresses without a special pump was too much for one day. She was tired, so she gave up and spread a clean sheet on the floor and lay down on it, clothes on, because she couldn't remember where she'd packed the blankets. It was too hot to do anything anyway.

She could hear the clatter of children playing outside, and it leaked into her dreams, and she dreamed that she was herself but had no son, she'd never had a son, never been pregnant. She woke up unsure where she was, blinking in the dim half-light from the parking lot, her clothes musty and too close to her skin. Usually, she would turn to Seth and say, *I had one of those dreams again*, but Seth wasn't there to say it to. Jessie turned over and hugged the toy lion to her chest.

Outside, she heard a toddler shriek. What time was it? Too late for children to be awake, certainly. A car door closed. She fell back into the gray space behind her eyes, and the next time she woke up, it was daytime, and she was sure she knew where she was and that the short, good period she'd shared with Seth was completely, fully over.

Before she left the truck in the driveway, the way Seth told her to, she twisted the keys around in her hand for a long time, fingering the square, thick key that said *Do Not Duplicate* on its bow. The lights were off in Seth's house, but that didn't mean he was at the job site. With these keys, Jessie could have let herself in one more time, stood in the kitchen, and looked out the window of the house she and her son had lived in before things fell apart all over again.

*     *     *

NEIL WAS BORN LIKE THIS, with a fatal flaw sewn through his developing lungs. He had been early—horribly, shockingly early. Before Jessie could even go into labor, a team of doctors transferred Neil out of her body and into a plastic uterus where he could finish growing. He had a breathing tube and a feeding tube. His father, Noah, sat by the incubator with his hand on the plastic. He looked at the red and green dots that Neil's wireless monitoring patch broadcast to the nearby screen. He looked at his phone. He didn't look at Jessie, who sat on the padded bench across the room, leaking milk through her shirt.

They both knew whose fault this was. The incubator was an upgrade, as far as Noah was concerned. It was reliable; Jessie was not. It was safe; Jessie was not. It delivered healthy babies; Jessie could not.

She watched Noah's hand stroke the shining bubble that covered their son; the plastic was infused with antibacterial and antibiotic chemicals that shielded Neil more effectively than her weak, human flesh. Neil moved like a little pink rabbit in a germ-proof hutch. He would have respiratory problems for the rest of his life, the doctor said. The feeding tube might eventually give way to something less invasive, but he'd need special occupational therapy in order to learn to swallow. He would have no sense of taste. His nose would have a permanent ridge from the breathing mask that pressed into his baby skin.

NOAH AND JESSIE WERE MARRIED for a year before Neil arrived. For their wedding, Noah, the aspiring theologian, had chosen Anglican vows:

*The union of husband and wife in heart, body, and mind is intended by God for their mutual joy; for the help and comfort given one another in prosperity and adversity; and, when it is God's will, for the procreation of children and their nurture in the knowledge and love of the Lord.*

He'd been reading G.K. Chesterton. Jessie thought her husband was progressive, and he probably thought he was too. It was easy to be open-minded when nothing was wrong and everything seemed straight and normal and they were just stupid kids, going to coffee after Sunday worship and getting dizzy on mocha espresso shakes. Noah was finishing his pastoral counseling certificate. He adopted the swinging, good-guy tones of a youth minister.

*You know who else was a righteous dude? The Risen Jesus.*

He dressed the part, too, favoring beachwear and often showing up to church in sandals. He wore collared shirts with Hawaiian flowers embroidered on them.

One of the things Jessie liked about Noah was that he preached acceptance. At first, he seemed to practice it. *Let Jesus in. God doesn't make junk.* His bookcases were swollen with copies of religious texts, spiritual writings, and diverse and exotic rituals. He liked to quote Alan Watts and Joseph Campbell and would sometimes weave a Johnny Cash lyric into his junior sermons—no: his "talks." He was supposed to have the confidence of experience, he told Jessie, but seem like a reliable, cool friend, someone people could come to with their struggles. Someone who was unbothered by his life and had no problems of his own.

Jessie felt that he was the key to her life. When he held her hand, she sensed the door of her future opening easily, lightly, although she'd battered herself against it alone for what seemed like ages. That's how it was, in Phoenix, Oregon. There were no gay people there; she'd only ever seen them on TV. She didn't yet have a word for what she was. With Noah in the picture, things started to get easier. People included her and remembered her name. She didn't make them nervous anymore. At church, she and Noah had "their" place, at the very front, although saving seats was discouraged and they renounced hierarchy every Sunday and told themselves they were equal under Christ. *The Lord doesn't play favorites.*

*Of course He does,* Jessie thought. *Otherwise, why bother trying to get on His good side?* She and Noah exchanged the sign of peace, feeling the congregation's eyes on them, assessing. She forgot to look at girls, she was so busy preparing to be a pastor's wife.

However, the desire was still in her, sleeping. She ignored it, hoping that, by the time she got married, that part of her would be gone. She acted the part and waited for the change to take place. The first time she was with Noah, on their wedding night, he was surprised by the blood on the condom.

"I didn't think you were a virgin," he said. "You don't kiss like one."

"I've never been with a man," she said, which was technically true. Only fingers and lips had explored her. She'd only been with girls, but as hard as she came for them, she believed and hoped in some deep part of herself that because they weren't guys it didn't count.

That first night, Noah tenderly kissed her belly. Jessie felt her lie take hold there and fester, like a bad seed. He wanted to believe she was untouched, so she let him. It was supposed to be a trade, because she wanted to stop falling in love with girls, stop thinking of their skin and thrusting tongues when her husband tried to give her the sanctified pleasure God designated for married people.

After a couple of months, she thought maybe she would tolerate marriage better if they had a baby. She asked Noah to make her pregnant, and he happily complied. She felt guilty that he was so in love with her. Really, he loved the story she'd let him believe about them, and it excited him to be the first man who ever touched her. He wanted to be her teacher. The condom came off, and still she felt nothing when he fucked her. She learned to make the right sounds to encourage him or console him when he couldn't finish inside her. It felt like the payment of a debt. Poor Noah.

That's why Neil had special needs. God withheld his favor because the marriage was incomplete, because of Jessie. Noah told Jessie he wanted three children. But after Neil, it was obvious that they couldn't try again. She was blighted; she made sick babies. God had not blessed their union. For this, Noah found it impossible to forgive her.

Jessie's sin was contagious, and she'd passed it to their child. Noah knew. He was afraid of her sinfulness. He got rough with her in bed and called her names. He wrapped her hair around his fist and pulled it hard. They said hateful words to each other. When she stopped sleeping in their bed, he curled up with his laptop instead, jerking off onto her half of the sheets and leaving the mess for her to find.

If sometimes she said out loud how bad she was, she felt better. Once, after Neil was born, Noah looked at her while she was trying to work the breast pump. The baby was asleep, and she needed to express and relieve the horrible pressure in her tits. She fumbled with the pump, saying it was her fault, all her fault, she'd moved wrong and that's why it wasn't working. Noah's expression stopped her dead.

"You're not *doing* anything," he said. "It's your nature. You can't help the way you are."

Right after Neil's second birthday, Jessie got tired of it and left for Portland: Queer City.

NOAH SENT A COUPLE HUNDRED bucks a month. The agreement was to stay married because that was better for insurance and also for Noah's job. He came up to Portland from Phoenix every couple of months, to be there for Neil's more serious doctor appointments. He missed them, he said. He missed Jessie. He was finding that it was easier to share the Gospel when life at home was loving and fulfilled. He put his hand on Jessie's knee in front of the pediatrician and he was still wearing his wedding ring: a hokey thing he'd chosen himself, bands carved from oak and antler.

He called every week, even though Neil couldn't talk yet and might not ever, even if he figured out chewing and swallowing. When Jessie stopped responding to his calls, he switched to texts and then just pictures: of himself; of her favorite coffee drink; of the church; of their old friends at band practice; of his penis, throttled purple by his hand. He sent a picture of the Phoenix sign, captioned *population 4,496 + 2 people who I wish would come home.*

Why the fuck would she call that place home? They were never going back. Noah told Jessie he was praying for her, and she knew that, if she wanted to get away from him, she'd have to go ahead and fuck somebody else. Not just anybody: someone who owned a dick.

Seth had one she could use.

She worked part-time at the Children's Hospital, in the cafeteria, and spent every spare moment upstairs with Neil in the respiratory ward. She was in her early twenties and still very pretty. She didn't wear her silver-plated cross anymore, or the big amethyst ring Noah gave her. She lived in an extended-stay hotel across from the hospital. With the "Good Samaritan" discount plus the money from Noah, she could afford it, week by week. She ate cafeteria food and drank coffee from the urn at work. She kept hoping that this, whatever *this* was, wasn't forever. She cut her hair short, a sensible length, and clipped it back with a plastic barrette, the kind she'd had when she was in grade school. She didn't look like an eager Christian, or a mother, or even like a grown-up. She was nothing, starting over as no one.

Seth said, when he finally took her to his house, that he'd assumed she was a dropout.

"Dropped out of what?" she'd asked. Her hand looked so small next to his. He kissed her fingers.

"You look like a runaway."

"Run away from what?" she pressed, but he didn't answer. The bees on the lavender bush outside buzzed in and out of his bedroom window like idle thoughts, dipping over their heads as they lay together, gathering nectar.

He understood her situation, or what she told him. He felt sorry about Neil, who was not even three and spending every other week at the Children's Hospital. Neil's life expectancy kept shrinking. He outgrew each prescription almost as soon as it started working. He was withering in the bell jar that was supposed to keep him safe.

The waiting made her crazy. She watched Neil's lungs slowly fill with sand. Some days, she wished he'd never been born; on others, she fantasized about strangling him or unplugging the machine that kept oxygen flowering in his blood. He'd spent his whole life packed in plastic. Two years and counting. She'd stopped believing in healing miracles and was just waiting for his term to be over. She wished he'd died in utero. She imagined lying on him and smothering him until he wasn't sick anymore.

Mothers weren't supposed to have those thoughts. And Seth's sympathy felt safe, like a place to hide from her worst self, a refuge. He was twice her age, secure. He worked construction, piecing together the many tall, sparkling towers of condos that sprouted up like saplings all over Portland.

When he helped move her boxes and bags out of her hotel room and into his truck, he joked that the load was like feathers, compared to the beams they lifted daily at work. He told her how small she was and light, nothing at all, not like the city he constructed around her. His job was remaking the garden of the world into a cage; hers was to admire what he built and celebrate her captivity.

Jessie told Seth everything except that she was probably gay and also not divorced yet. Eden only had room for two people: a mating pair of humans. So that was the price you paid for living there: You couldn't tell men that you didn't love them *like that*. But you had to leave, after a while, even though they loved you and would do anything to make you change your mind. Even though your son would be sick again, and more often, you couldn't sacrifice your body for his; you had to leave, because something in you was broken and no matter how sorry you were, you just didn't belong in paradise.

Those were the rules. That's how Eden worked.

\*   \*   \*

JESSIE OPENED EVERY WINDOW AND the front door of her new apartment to try to air out the stink of cat piss and cigarettes. Even with their bodies cloaked in black abayas, Jessie could see that some of her neighbors were pregnant. Having babies was a holy commandment: the body of God called out of your body, to multiply His message on earth. Every religion said as much, which is how they'd all managed to propagate themselves so efficiently.

Neil might never live here with her, but she set up his room anyway, arranging his stuffed animals on his bed in a friendly receiving line. She plugged in the various filters, masks, and breathing machines and turned them on. The familiar hiss relaxed her. *Home is where your respirator is.* It didn't take long to open the rest of the boxes and put her few dishes, pans, and books away. She didn't have any furniture, aside from the twin inflatable mattresses Seth had bought her at an outdoor store.

"How is it possible you've never been camping?" he'd teased her. He picked out solar lamps and a shower that could be rigged up in a tree while she examined pods of dehydrated meals. They were probably worse than they looked.

"I wasn't raised like that. The only reason anyone sleeps outside is that they're not allowed in the house," she said. He thought that was funny.

"You'll love the mountains," he'd said.

They didn't make it that far. Now, she was across town, and her landscape was not exactly picturesque. On her walk to check the mailbox, she noticed a lavender plant pushing a fistful of stems out of the mulch in a concrete planter. She was tempted to take some: just one flower, pinched between her fingers, would bring back the smell of Seth's garden and all the easy times she'd had there. Instead, she jammed her mail key into the rusty lock and felt inside, even though it was too soon to get mail, even flimsy circulars with coupons to clip for dental whitening and thin crust pizza. She slapped the door shut and, mad at herself for expecting anything to change at her behest, wrenched the key out, stepped back, and collided full-on with a woman she didn't realize was standing right behind her. Jessie's elbow connected with the woman's belly, which was full and pregnant, solid as a watermelon.

They both screamed.

"Sorry, sorry," Jessie said, reaching for the woman, who moved back, covering her belly with her hands. "Are you all right? I'm so sorry, I didn't see you. Are you hurt? I'm sorry."

She babbled, knew she was babbling. The woman stared at her.

Maybe she didn't speak English.

Jessie put her hands over her own belly, where Neil was briefly housed, and frowned. The woman's expression did not change. She turned on her heel and walked away, so heavy with her pregnancy that she swayed from side to side. Jessie watched her climb the stairs and heard a door slam: This was her downstairs neighbor.

She waited a minute, then followed. She felt a terrible pang, a stabbing guilt that squeezed her stomach. What if she'd hurt the baby? What if the woman went into labor? What if she'd broken some Muslim taboo and created a problem she knew nothing about? She tiptoed up the steps and held her breath as she went past the woman's door. She could not detect any movement or sound inside, not even the noise of a TV or radio. She went into her own apartment and carefully closed the door. She wondered, for the first time, if the woman downstairs could hear her footsteps overhead and if that was a disturbance.

She took the bus to work, leaving earlier than she needed to. Every car in the apartment complex parking lot had Lyft and Uber stickers on its windows. The cars, spotless black Hondas and Hyundais with seat covers, were as identical as a fleet of real taxis. The bus, in contrast, was filthy and smelled like weed, feet, and wet laundry. Jessie sat by the window with the screen vented open even though it was bitingly cold.

The heater blasted her feet until she could barely feel them. She served two of the day's menus, visited Neil, and went home.

And then, the same thing again. And again. Again. Six days a week, six hours a day. Only full-time employees got health benefits, and every week she was scheduled two hours short. Her day off was Friday. She didn't sleep in. She caught the bus and brought Neil a coloring book in the morning.

Intent, only partially understanding, he watched her trace the princesses with a crayon. Oxygen deprivation affects every system in the body, from the brain to the cellular ganglia. The whole body needs to breathe: Without air, its parts die slowly, one at a time. They shrink. Neil, a compassionate nurse once explained to Jessie, was choking, gradually, in the very gentlest possible way.

Jessie had heard in church about death by crucifixion, when Noah told the congregation it was *excruciating*. Even the two words had the same roots. Stretched to death, nailed up. On Good Friday, he gave a scientific sermon about the torture and death of Christ. He explained how the lack of oxygen in the Lord's blood would collapse his blood vessels one at a time, allowing fluid to diffuse into the tissues of his body, including the lungs and the sac around the heart. Death by drowning. Sac. *Sacred.* She colored in a crown and a bridal veil. Neil took the crayon from her, and she let him. His hands were hot and stiff. He scribbled over the princess's face, dropped the crayon, and screamed when it rolled off his bed onto the floor.

Jessie retrieved it.

"See?" She blocked in some of the shapes he'd scrawled.

Now the princess was wearing a CPAP mask. She held up the drawing, and he bapped it. She didn't think of him as knowing what he looked like, or able to comprehend his own reflection in a mirror. At least the picture made him laugh. She stayed until afternoon meds, then kissed him, sang him his favorite alphabet song, and tucked him in. She zippered the vinyl tent around the bed and turned the lights off as she left his room. He spent so little time away from the hospital that he slept poorly in other beds, in rooms with different sounds and smells. Seth's fountain lulled him, but that was all a dream now, an experience Neil wouldn't remember. She'd taken her son there knowing it could not last, would not heal him, could never change what was wrong with either of them.

Neil was susceptible to fevers and agues, which came over him like possession and had to be cast out with antibiotics and special tanks of flavored air. During these periods, Jessie was banished and sent back to normal, oxygenated life. She was unusually aware of heat and wind in these times: the clouds of steam that came out of the chafing dishes at work, the stove's flame that greedily sucked air into its blue corona, and the cigarette haze that seemed to follow her when she walked past the people smoking at the bus stop. Rain touched her less, when Neil was sick. She always seemed to be waiting.

A month passed.

At the new apartment, she paced. She opened and closed windows. She bleached the bathtub and disinfected every surface. Her hands were saturated with the smell of Lysol wipes. Seth didn't text, which was fine. Cleaning distracted her from herself and made her feel better, in control. She didn't want anything *living* in her new space, not cut flowers or a cactus or even ants investigating the baseboards in the kitchen. She found a black smear that might possibly have been mold in the bathroom behind the toilet and was kneeling down, ferociously scrubbing the ever-loving, almighty shit out of the grout, when she heard a tiny scream.

She dropped the sponge and flinched, smacking her ear against the ceramic tank. Her head buzzed. Maybe she was wrong, imagined it. The sound. The shriek. Again.

The cry, both irregular and inconsolable, was worse than the piercing wail of a cat. A newborn baby was screaming in the apartment downstairs.

She lay on the bathroom floor and listened. She could hear someone down there, talking or singing. Water running. Feet. Then, more crying. More. Each scream sent shivers through Jessie's body; she remembered Neil making that sound and the way she'd resented her body's instinctive obedience to his imperious demands. Her nipples had beaded with milk if she even *thought* about Neil, early on. She'd ruined every bra she owned. If he snuffled or even whimpered, her breasts ballooned. The only thing she could do was pump and pump and save it all for later. She spent hours sitting next to Neil's antibacterial baby pod, gazing at him and listening to one machine put breath in him while another one took milk from her.

She'd hated it.

The baby downstairs howled, and Jessie heard another voice crying too. Those uneven, exhausted sobs—she knew that sound. She'd made it a few times herself.

The woman downstairs was not holding the baby when she answered the door. She had gray circles under her eyes and her head was uncovered. Her hair, pulled back in a bun, was greasy at the roots and dyed deep auburn. She was wearing cotton-candy-pink sweatpants and a loose, stained T-shirt covered in Minnie Mouses. Without her abaya, she looked young, not much older than Jessie.

"I'm sorry about the baby," she said. "She won't eat and she's exhausted."

"You both are."

"I hope it doesn't disturb you."

"No. May I come in? To help?"

The woman looked her over and nodded, stepping back. Jessie slipped off her shoes. She heard another shriek, louder now that she was inside, and she felt the old adrenaline rush start to kick up. She washed her hands with conspicuous care, twice, and dried them on a paper towel. The woman came back into the kitchen with the infant, who was shivering with rage. Its tiny hands clawed the woman's skin and shoulders, scraping her with nails as flimsy as Bible paper. Its yellow duck onesie was new and crisp looking, as though it had been ironed; it wore matching socks. A tiny tyrant in a tutu.

"She just cries," the woman said. "Do you have kids?"

"My son."

Jessie got a glass from the dish rack, filled it at the sink, and pointed to the sofa in the living room. They sat down, deafened by the baby.

The woman murmured and tried to soothe it. Jessie remembered pantomiming this same performance for the lactation aide, petting and singing to Neil when she would have liked to jump out of the hospital window with him clutched screaming in her arms. They'd land in the trees; at least it would be quiet.

The woman looked at her, humiliated. "She cries."

Jessie smiled in empathy. "My son was like that too. She won't eat?"

The woman lifted her shirt and held the baby against her chest. It nuzzled her but didn't latch on. The woman bent over it, crooning. Her left breast, uncovered, began to seep.

"Help," she said. "I'm so tired."

Without thinking, Jessie reached out and touched the woman's bosom, lifted it. The first bead of milk slipped down over the tight, curving flesh and drizzled across Jessie's hand.

"Put her on this side," Jessie said. Together, they adjusted the baby. Jessie took a pillow from the sofa and stuck it under the woman's arm for support.

"She's going to cry."

Jessie touched the woman again, clasping her nipple between her first two fingers and pulling it gently out. The woman hugged her baby, and its mouth connected with a stream of milk. The latching-on was instant: always so fierce, that survival instinct and the animal-fast reflexes inside even a week-old, unformed body. The baby clicked and sucked. Its mother—*her* mother, this was a girl, or could be someday—relaxed. Jessie handed her the glass of water.

"I always got thirsty when I did this," she said.

The baby's head was warm and sweet-smelling, surprisingly heavy. She'd forgotten how big babies were, how their presence was intoxicating. Like alcohol or God, babies changed the laws of nature; the rules didn't apply.

"Then I do the other side, same way?"

Jessie nodded. "Did the nurse show you, in the hospital?"

"There wasn't one. And honestly," the woman said, her voice suddenly tangy, "honestly, do I need another white person telling me what to do? My usual doctor wasn't there, and the one they gave me assumed I was Arab."

"Jesus."

"If one more person tells me how good my English is, or asks any stupid questions, I am going to lose my mind. One nurse tried to make sure she pushed my wheelchair five feet behind my husband when we took Sariah out to the car seat, because she thought that's what good Muslim wives do. Walk behind! And they asked if a family member was going to bring a cab!"

She laughed, but it wasn't funny. The baby let go of her nipple, and she looked down at it, dazed, as though she'd forgotten what her body had been doing all this time.

Jessie nodded. She patted the sofa cushion and asked, "Ready for the other side?"

"She'll probably sleep after this, right?"

"I hope so. And you too."

She reached for the woman's other breast, uncovered it, and stroked the milk into it, coaxing its tissues to perform their natural calling. The woman started to sing again, quietly, and to Jessie's surprise it wasn't a psalm or holy chant, as she'd assumed, but a song from *The Little Mermaid* about kissing the girl and making the most of the moment at hand. Jessie, to her surprise, remembered this one. The tune popped into her mouth. She hummed along with the parts she knew, *sha la, don't be so shy,* and she felt the mother and child responding to each other, turning inward to fulfill some private, divine purpose, the passing of life from one to another without will or resistance or even love. She held them both, though they didn't need her. They had a way all laid out for them: They knew it was meant to be.

# DOMESTIC SHORTHAIR

AMANDA WASN'T EVEN PRETTY, BUT she knew how to work it. Leaning in the bathroom doorway, I watched while she applied her makeup for yet another Tinder date. Her nose, too heavy for her heart-shaped face, got a couple lines of contour. She combed her eyebrows with a tiny dry-mascara brush and penciled them. For a casual first date, she didn't put on the individual fake lashes, which looked to me like disembodied tarantula legs preserved in a plastic vanity bubble. She was a lot shorter than me, and I could see the sandy roots of her natural hair color coming in. She took out a powder puff and blended the layers and lines, making a smooth mask that was both just like her face and nothing like it at all.

"How am I doing?" she said, pressing her lips together.

"What're you wearing? The black top again?"

She blinked, exaggerating her eyes like a doll's. "Probably. And my boots."

Men loved those boots, and she knew it. She called them her *catnip*: fake Louboutins whose red soles were peeling off. They gave her about four or five inches and made her walk with a sexy swivel, totally different than the heavy kitchen clogs she wore for work every day.

"Breaking out the big guns?"

"Hardly. Anyway, he's cute. And tall. Take a peek."

I picked her phone up off the vanity and put in the passcode. She had the app open to his photo. Six-foot-five, green eyes, athletic build. A man of few words, from the bio. Probably stupid.

"He looks like your type," I said. I flicked through the photos: man with three similar-looking friends; man in sports jersey; man holding someone else's baby; man with fish—the usual. "Does he eat carbs?"

"I don't date boys who don't eat carbs." She turned to pluck the phone from my hand. She whisked the makeup brush across the tip of my nose. "Seriously, Amit, you should come out sometime. All you do is work."

I went into the kitchen without answering her and turned on the stove even though I didn't really want to drink tea. I was on the schedule for that night, actually, but hadn't mentioned it to Amanda. I didn't like coming home after the night shift and smelling her sex through the apartment. She brought these men over on the first night, left lipstick stains on my wine glasses, let them sleep in her bed until late morning. Once I stopped telling her when I was going to be gone, though, there were no more mystery guests. That was our unwritten agreement: She could fuck whomever she wanted, but not where I could hear it.

"Would you zip me?"

She trotted after me, heels clicking on the bamboo floor tiles. She turned around and presented me with her bare back. She was scented with Chanel Mademoiselle and baby powder. *Catnip.* The zipper teeth were jammed, so I picked at the seam until it loosened, then eased the tab up.

"This is getting tight," I said. "It was baggy on you a few weeks ago."

"I think I put it in the dryer by accident," she said, pushing her bleached hair over her shoulders. She styled it in crispy curls. Her selfies were fabulous, and when I saw her all made up like this, I noticed the components of her face that made her so striking: the wide-set eyes, bow lips, and delicate brows. Men, she told me once, didn't notice subtle things like artificial cosmetic colors or shapes. They couldn't differentiate between an unnatural blush and a real one; all they knew was that they liked it. Amanda knew it. Amanda could work it.

"I can't believe you don't eat everything in sight at the restaurant," I said. "I would weigh a ton."

"My last date told me I smelled like apple pie." She winked at me over her shoulder, took her bag, and checked her phone. "My Uber's here. Maybe I'll see you tomorrow."

"Be safe," I said, like always, like it ever made a difference.

\*     \*     \*

I HAVE PERFECTED THE ART of acting straight. In locker rooms or when I'm shopping or even on the street, I know how to talk to women in a way that suggests: *I am like you* and *I am not a threat*. The best way to do it is to sweeten my voice, make it higher, and offer compliments that include the words *so cute*. I always mention my boyfriend, who is an imaginary person, or my partner, who doesn't exist unless I close my eyes, and I see Amanda, taking up the whole bathroom or leaving her clogs in the middle of the floor, or scrolling through the Humane Society website and crying because of all the kittens nobody will adopt, or forgetting to put the groceries away so that the frozen things all melt into separate lumps in their plastic and cardboard containers, or making my bed for me as a surprise and leaving a handful of pansies in the middle of it, or feeding me a bite of buttercream frosting on the end of her special icing spatula. For six years, I've come home to her. Both of our names are on the mailbox.

MY IMAGINARY BOYFRIEND IS TALLER than me and doesn't mind that I look like a dyke. He likes tomboys, I tell the girl changing next to me in the locker room, trying to keep my eyes away from her. *Mine's like that too*, she says, as though commiserating. *I wish I could just let myself get fat, quit the gym*. Acting straight means nodding when women describe the lengths they go to catch a man, keep him, and please him.

This stranger popped her breasts out of her sports bra practically in my face because we didn't see each other. When I act straight, my personal space disappears. Men touch me without asking. Women don't mind standing too close to me. Erasing myself seems like a small price to pay for feeling less alone.

Amanda is the only one who knows, because there is no way I can keep up this performance all the time. Acting straight is tiring, and, when I come home and flop onto the couch, I can feel those behaviors leaving me, one at a time.

"You're an alto," she told me when she first moved in. "Your voice."

"Maybe I have a cold," I said, but she didn't bring it up again.

I used my straight woman behavior at work, too, because it put the victims at ease. Police procedure was stressful enough; did they really need another thing to worry about while I scanned their bodies with the black light and swabbed for samples in their most protected places? The only place I wasn't straight, aside from home, was on my dating profile.

*   *   *

WHEN AMANDA WAS GONE, I logged in and flicked through the profiles of women who were supposed to match with me. Were they queer the same way I was? None of them looked like me. The gay girls were all short, under five-foot-four, and I couldn't imagine leaning down to kiss one of them. They were child-sized. I couldn't touch one without thinking about work, the businesslike handling of underage bodies and children with scabbed knees. The trauma stuck to me like the scent of rubbing alcohol. I tried short girls sometimes, because there were so many of them, but I couldn't make myself get interested. I didn't know exactly what I was looking for, but whoever it was needed to feel *substantial* in my mind. I didn't want a lover who fit in my lap. I didn't want to feel like anyone's mother.

Nobody on the app caught my fancy, though I had a few messages. They were all the same. I read each one without responding. One of my fears was that I would see someone I recognized, someone from the lab or, even worse, one of the victims or one of their family members, that they would find my profile, with its clear-cut orientation and the "don't let straight people see me" box checked, and suddenly realize that the gloved hand that slid the speculum into them for Exam Group A tests was not a straight woman's hand, or even really a woman's hand, although the way I was built suggested *lady, female.* I learned a long time ago that giving people the words they need in order to know how to treat me was important. I am physically female, but I am not a woman. I am not attracted to men, though I do not hate them or find them repulsive. I avoid pronouns when I refer to myself or others. I have an ambiguous name, short for nothing. The messages usually ask about it, but I can't say anything intelligent; there isn't anything to say.

IN THE BATHROOM, I PICKED up Amanda's toothbrush and pressed the tip of my tongue to its bristles. Her toothpaste, different from mine, crackled over my taste buds. Maybe her date was inhaling her breath right now, getting her lipstick on his face. Straight women don't have these thoughts. They cheerfully toss their shiny ponytails and go to bed with a bounce in their steps, thinking, *Gee, I hope she's having fun.* When they say "girlfriend" it means something different from when I say "girlfriend." The cord to Amanda's hair dryer protruded from the drawer, a tangled black plastic vine. I tried to shove it back and, as I did, my eye fell on a long white box with the Clearblue logo on it: advanced pregnancy test, rapid results. The box was open; one of the two plastic sticks was already used. I didn't see it in the trash; she must have taken it at work. I shook out the other test and looked down into the blank window. Women saw their futures in these things.

When I touched anything of hers, I put it back exactly the way I found it. If she had something to share with me, she would. Until then, I just collected the evidence. I knew she only lived with me because she couldn't afford to live alone. She had a whole life, separate from mine. That didn't stop me from loving her.

\*　　\*　　\*

23

I WAS MOSTLY SWING SHIFT at the lab, four days on and two off. Technically I was part of the Portland Police Association even though I'd never even shot a gun. I explained this to Amanda once, and she just nodded.

"You look like a cop," she said.

"What's that?"

"I mean, you look like a cop *should* look. Serious. Trustworthy. Not a real cop."

"I'm not a real cop."

"There you go."

SHE WAS THE PASTRY CHEF at a nice restaurant downtown, a fancy bistro that printed a separate dessert menu with her name at the top. She made banana cream pie with chocolate caramel sauce, tiramisu and mousse, and panettone with bergamot marmalade. She cooked a lot at home, too, mostly overnight sourdough pancakes and little cookies, the kind ladies have with their tea. Our place smelled like heaven, like powdered sugar and Meyer lemon mixed together in sweet almond paste. One time she made a whole tray of cream puffs filled with huckleberry cream and glazed with honey, sprinkled with bee pollen and raw sugar—fairy food.

"Nobody at the lab's going to appreciate these," I said. I held one between my thumb and finger. It shone with sweetness. My mouth watered.

"But I made them for you. You can just leave them in the break room. Come on," she said.

"What am I going to say?"

She pressed a sheet of wax paper into a shallow Tupperware container. "Don't say anything, then. Just say your friend made them."

My *friend*.

"I guess it's more of a pie and coffee kind of place, right?" She picked up the first puff with a pair of tiny silver tongs and nestled it into the box. "There are forty-two of these. We can't eat all of them."

I ate the one I had taken and stuffed my sticky hands in my pockets. She was biting her lip, the way she did when somebody had hurt her feelings. "I'll take them, okay? They're perfect. You didn't have to do this."

"I wanted to. Quit acting like I'm nice."

But she was, mostly, nice. I think that's why it worked out. In bed, before I went to sleep, I added up the nice things she had said and done and thought of how I could possibly repay her. She wouldn't like that— me keeping count—but that's just the way it worked. The special cream puffs were gone by the first coffee break on my shift.

"What were those, Amit?" my manager Jeff asked. "Blueberry?"

"Huckleberry."

"Amazing," he said, and kissed his fingers, making them explode from his lips like a firework. "Whoever says that food isn't love is missing out."

Later that morning, I did a basic kit on a dazed seventeen-year-old girl who'd been roofied at a party and then sodomized by the friend she thought was going to take her home. I held her hand and scraped under her nails, trying to capture any hair, skin, or other DNA that might be trapped there. She leaned toward me while I wiggled the curved manicure tool against her nail bed.

"I'm almost through," I said. "I'm sorry I can't be more gentle."

"You smell like magic donuts." She leaned her head on my shoulder. I wasn't supposed to, but I let her stay there until the sample was done.

AMANDA'S DATE WITH THE MOST recent Tinder guy was probably fine, because I didn't hear from her until late the next morning when she texted me from the restaurant.

*You should come get coffee and I'll give you one of the scones I'm working on,* she said.

I replied, *Twist my arm.*

\*    \*    \*

WHEN SHE BROUGHT THE TINY white plate and the cup on its pearly saucer to my two-top in the corner, I noticed that she had gained weight. She was thicker through her arms, and her waist was starting to disappear. She was tying her apron higher than usual.

"I know, I need to go shopping," she said when she saw me eyeing her. "My jeans don't fit. I should quit eating at work so much."

"You could borrow mine, but you'd have to cuff them."

"You're like a foot taller than me! And anyway, I love shopping."

I hate shopping. But I nodded and offered to go with her on my next day off. Because it wouldn't be a hassle or anything, and I could drive, I said. The scone was delicious. She'd smeared it with sage butter. I pressed the crumbs with my fingertip and ferried them to my mouth.

AT THE SECONDHAND STORE, SHE picked out three pairs of dark Dickies, work pants, and a vintage silk blouse that hung on her like a tent. Usually, she spun around in front of me or at least clucked to me from the fitting room about how something looked. *You like this top? It looks like something my dad would wear.* But this time, she walked straight to the cashier's station with her arms full of clothes, plopped them on the counter, and pulled out her wallet. I was bending up the brim of a funny-looking felt hat when she called to me from the doorway.

"You're ready to go?"

"I knew what I wanted. Plus, it doesn't matter if they're not flattering, it's just for work."

"Not that shirt, though."

She smiled, the first real one I'd seen on her in a while. "I'm taking a few days off next week. I'm due for a mini vacation. That guy from Tinder wants to take me to the coast."

"Fun," I said. I didn't say: *Most of the stories I hear at work start that way.* I didn't ask for his full name or even his address because I knew that Amanda didn't keep track of things like that. I didn't tell her about the woman I ran a test kit for last month, whose "boyfriend" shot her up on Dilaudid and sold her to a bachelor party. I didn't tell Amanda that, when blood is mixed with the sample, it makes it difficult to isolate a single attacker's DNA.

She saw my expression, though. "Amit. It's just two nights. He's fine."

"I didn't say anything."

"You did, though. You did."

WE GOT A HAMBURGER AT Mel's on the way home, and I let her eat my fries. She looked at her phone the whole time, not really talking to me. In the corner, above the milkshake machine, a small monitor played the TV-edited version of *Runaway Bride*. Julia Roberts' smile filled the square screen; her mouth was like a shark's, so wide I expected to see more than one row of white teeth.

"Where on the coast?"

"Just let it go, Amit. I'll text you so that you know he hasn't dismembered me. When I get home, it's back-to-back weddings and banquets. I need a break."

I went back to my burger. Amanda's fingers darted into the red plastic basket, removing one fry at a time. Julia Roberts laced up her running shoes.

"I'm going to miss you, that's all," I muttered.

I am positive she didn't hear me.

*       *       *

ALMOST FOUR WEEKS WENT BY when all I saw of Amanda were her dishes in the rack and her three pairs of sensible pants rumpled on top of the washing machine. She did text, sometimes, mostly about how she needed another vacation after that last one with what's-his-face. She was rhapsodic about his shortcomings, which I think was mostly to make me feel better. She told me how work was and how the sous put in his notice without telling anyone in the kitchen and how they'd caught one of the waiters secretly drinking the triple sec. She shared all the gossip. This was her way of making up to me when she knew she'd done something that rubbed me the wrong way. She never said she was sorry, exactly. She just gave me more of her attention.

*Amaretto or vanilla bean?* she texted.

*For what? Cake?*

*Angel food that isn't boring.*

That was my cue to jump in with a joke, about angels or sponges or *something*, but I'd just swabbed semen from the rectum of a four-year-old boy and I wasn't in the mood. I clicked my phone off and set it screen-down on the break room table.

Jeff sat down across from me. "You want a coffee?"

"No. Just a minute."

Because of the job, the nature of it, we weren't expected to adhere too strictly to the employment law-mandated break structure. Anyone who worked there for more than a year got used to the chronic emotional exhaustion. One hour into your shift, you might feel the floor start to fall out from under you. Or it could be that, after ten days on call, when the slideshow of images, of pink meat, and scared faces, and endlessly folding the white exam sheets, and emulsions of body fluids, and the sudden pressure of their hand over yours when it hurts, and the March 2008 issue of *People* magazine in the waiting room that nobody reads, and the tools, and the inspiring flower poster, and the quiet, the absolute quiet of someone who has been silenced by what's happened to them, catches you up in its zero-gravity suck and suddenly you are the one upside-down, sitting in the break room and staring at the square green digits on the microwave clock while they reorient themselves into different shapes that mean different times.

"Those little donuts you brought in that one time," said Jeff. "Those were good."

I rubbed my eyes. "My roommate made them."

"Really good," he repeated. "How long have you two lived together?"

"Six years. She's a pastry chef. Those were cream puffs, she was testing the recipe for work."

"Six years, and she can cook like that!"

I smiled at him. "She's great."

"Definitely a keeper," Jeff said. His eyes were on mine, full of secret messages. "Amit and Amanda, that's cute."

I sat back in my chair and slid my phone into my lap. "Thanks," I said.

"You ever think about having kids?"

"Not really."

He wiped his hands on his thighs. "She sure can cook." He got up from his chair.

Why didn't I correct him? I thought about all the things I could have said. But why should I set things straight? Maybe I didn't want to.

ALMOST ANOTHER WEEK PASSED BEFORE I saw Amanda again.

"I'm so fucking tired," she said. She drew the black liner over her lashes, making a cat-eye shape. "I look like Amy Winehouse."

"In a good way, right?" I said. I wanted to linger while she made herself up, which was our custom, but this time I couldn't make myself watch.

"I'll be back tonight, unless I like him," she called after me.

"Sounds good," I said and closed my door on the jangle of her phone.

ANOTHER WEEK PASSED WITH FEWER texts. I scrolled through our old conversations, wondering when I'd said the wrong thing.

I logged into the dating app more often and actually responded to a few messages. I skipped the crossdressers and the obviously straight men who'd changed their orientation on their profile so that they could harass people who were queer. (Report, block.)

*You have such beautiful eyes.* They told me that. They asked if I modeled, since I was tall. *What are you doing this weekend?* So many questions. I said I wasn't great at checking my messages and asked to meet for a drink instead. Amanda told me I was much more interesting in person and I believed her.

"You're magnetic," she told me once, when I asked her what made her want to move in. "And I knew I could trust you."

"How did you know that?"

29

"Can't I?" She had smiled, teasing me.

She had to know, by now.

SATURDAY, I CAME HOME FROM a date, and she was sitting in the living room in front of the TV, wrapped in a blanket. She didn't look up when I said hello.

"Are you feeling okay?" I asked. "You don't even like this show."

"I'll watch it in my room."

She stood up, still cocooned, and stumbled out. I heard her door slam. She'd left the television on so I could watch the *Game of Thrones* knights eviscerate one another. I sank into the warm spot on the cushions and stared at the screen until the swords and bare winter trees blurred together. I thought she might come back later or get a glass of water from the kitchen, but she didn't. I fell asleep on the sofa and didn't wake up until I heard her leaving for work.

"Amanda," I croaked, but she was gone.

ANOTHER WEEK WENT BY. I sent Amanda a picture of a cat eating a slice of birthday cake, but she didn't respond. I found her dirty dishes in the sink, or a pot on the stove with mashed potatoes drying on it. There were little white takeout boxes in the refrigerator. The bathroom smelled like her hairspray, but she was out of the house every morning by five. I considered setting my alarm and trying to catch her, but decided that if she wanted to avoid me, I'd let her.

If she wanted to move out, what would I even say about it? The reason *I* wanted her to stay wasn't her reason for not leaving. She didn't have the money. Even as a top pastry chef, she didn't make enough to live on her own. She couldn't leave, not without a reference. No, she wouldn't leave like this. I wondered if she'd meet someone else, move in with him. How I would react when she told me. These are the things I thought about when I drove to the police station for my shift. Jeff saw me lingering by the coffeemaker and asked if things were okay at home. I couldn't answer.

"Women," he said, commiserating.

I only nodded and looked miserably into my mug, as though the answers were floating in it.

Finally, on Monday evening, I knocked on her door.

"I'm going out," I said. "I have a date."

"Have fun," she said.

"Can I come in?"

I held my breath, counted.

"Sure."

I turned the knob. A white votive candle was lit by her bed, but the lights were off. The room smelled sour, a rancid combination of vanilla and wet socks. She was sitting up in bed; her tablet was a glowing rectangle beside her. Entering, I saw the stacks of plates and dirty dishes on the floor. Her clothes tumbled out of the closet in a dark wad that I had to step over as I came closer.

"You can sit on the bed," she said.

"Are you all right?" I settled on the corner of the mattress and turned toward her. She looked thinner and tired. "You've been working a lot."

"It's nonstop banquets. I always have something that's falling behind. You know how it is."

"I missed seeing you."

She shrugged. "Yeah. Well. You've had plenty going on."

"I went on *one* date."

"I'm just saying. I'm not the only one who's busy."

As we talked, her hands crept like crabs across the covers and gripped them compulsively. Her phone blipped at her, but she didn't move, not even to look at the notification.

"Amanda?"

She blinked, turned her face toward me. "I'm tired."

"I see that."

"Amit, I had an abortion."

My throat closed. I wanted to reach for her, put my fingers over hers, but I couldn't move. Her voice was low, rough. I realized that she had been crying.

"The clinic gave me some painkillers for after, but I hurt so much. I can barely stand. I almost fainted at work, from the pain."

"How long?"

"What?"

I swallowed. "When did you do this?"

"Four days ago."

And then all my words came out: "I would have taken you. Helped. Why didn't you tell me? You couldn't trust me with this?"

"Amit," she said, but it didn't stop me.

"Do you even know who the father was? Did you tell him? Who drove you home, after?"

She covered her face with her hands and stroked her straw-colored bangs back from her forehead. Even in the half-light, I could see how damaged her hair was. "Why does it matter? It's not like I was going to keep it. I'm not even dating anyone, why would I have a baby? I was in the second trimester, anyway. What am I going to do, text someone I fucked five months ago and let him know that he's going to be a father?"

"Five months? Jesus."

"It's expensive. I had to save up for the procedure. I couldn't take time off work. Stop looking at me like that. I could feel it moving, Amit. Do you know what that's like? *Moving.*"

"I would have helped you."

She snorted. "I don't want your help, Amit. I know how you are."

"How am I, exactly?"

The candles flickered as she waved her hand in front of her face. "It's hard with you. You can't just be there; it means too much. I took a cab home."

"I would have driven you."

She laughed, a dry little meow. "Yeah, you would have driven me home and put me in bed and all. I bet that, if I wanted to keep it, you'd want to help with that too. Help me pick out a name for it and everything. I'm not your pet. I don't belong to you."

I stood up. My stomach, my whole body was shaking. "It's your choice," I said. "I should go to bed, it's late."

"Don't dream about me, Amit."

And I didn't, that night. I couldn't sleep. I did the dishes as quietly as I could and stacked them on the drying rack. If Amanda heard the water running or the clinking ceramic and metal, she didn't get up to check on me. The pots were coated with experimental caramels, brittles, and syrups. She'd left a mess in the sink: a baking tin crusted with paper wrappers and burnt muffins; a handful of yellow flowers; strawberry cores covered in ants. I scrubbed a pie cutter: Its curved, silver blade was gummed with buttery flakes and cherry glue. As unsavory as this residue was, I still had the urge to taste it, to raise a soggy handful of crust to my mouth. *Soap, salt, cinnamon, sugar.* Amanda and her fanciful ingredients.

When I finished, it was well past midnight. The streetlights were on. I stood on the back porch with the pie cutter in my hand. The grass was getting long. Dandelions straggled across the lawn. Their powdery scent mingled with the sweet smell of the neighbor's pear tree. Once, we'd planned to have a garden. Amanda wanted herbs, and I wanted her to pick them: bouquets of mint, violets, thyme, and nasturtium. The garden was a fantasy that we talked over on snowy days when nothing was alive. When spring came, we didn't plant together. We were never home at the same time.

It didn't seem right to start without her.

I walked down the porch steps and dug the pie knife into the grass. The turf resisted me, but I hacked into it. The roots tore with a sound like capillaries breaking inside flesh. I chopped at them, then dropped the knife and started to yank the grass out with my hands. I didn't want to be in love with her anymore. The cool soil adhered to my fingers. I held up a clot of dirt and squinted at it, checking for worms, checking for sand and signs of viability. I looked for what I'd missed. *Evidence.*

\*     \*     \*

33

SHE DIDN'T MOVE OUT, BUT she didn't talk to me for a month, maybe longer. All I got was the Venmo notification when she paid her part of the rent and utilities. She put her makeup in a big case and kept it in her room instead of getting ready where I could see her. She kept away from me, and I hardly heard her coming home or leaving. I left her mail by her bedroom door and watched it pile up, then disappear, like autumn leaves. The sink refilled with dishes. There were no more pregnancy tests or even tampons, so I assumed she'd gotten an IUD.

Not that her choices were my business.

But then, I was on a break at work, and she texted me a picture of a husky with hearts over its eyes. The bubble coming out of its mouth said, *Let's get fat!*

I hesitated for a moment, then wrote back: *How about ice cream. Saturday?*

Yes, that worked. We had a date. I didn't realize that I'd been holding my breath. I exhaled and put my phone face down.

SHE WAS OUT OF THE house on Friday night, doing who knows what with God knows who. She came home while I was making coffee the next morning. The neighbor had started his leaf blower. When Amanda came in, she brought a burst of dust and noise with her that dissipated when she slammed the door. She dropped her overnight bag on the rug and kicked off her fake Louboutins. Immediately, she shrank back to her normal size, transforming from a femme fatale to her usual self. As she headed into the bathroom, she called, "Is that coffee?"

"I'll make you a cup," I said.

She emerged after a few minutes, her face damp and pale, traces of eyeliner still on her lids. As she poured cream into her mug of coffee, I noticed a bruise on the back of her hand, right over the primary metatarsal. The mark was curved and so faintly lavender that I almost missed it.

"What's this?" I asked, reaching for her.

She let me touch her. I rotated her wrist and checked for a hematoma. The bruise was less than twelve hours old and showed distinct patterning: a bite. Those were teeth marks. I dropped her hand as though it had burned me.

"Calm down, Amit. I gave much worse than I got."

"I don't want to know," I muttered. I took my coffee and went out on the back porch.

She followed me.

"What happened to the grass?" she asked. "Is that my pie cutter?"

Of course it was her pie cutter. Of course something happened to the grass. I eyed her. She seemed happier than usual, lighter. She stretched in the sun, tasted her coffee. "It's so nice to *not* be at work," she said.

"No more brunches?"

"I'm done for a while. Wedding season is next, and I'm dreading it. All those brides. All those cakes."

"You love it," I said.

She smiled. "It's a complex love."

She tucked her hair behind her ear. Her curls were still stiff in places and fraying loose hairs in others. A hairpin dangled, shaken loose of her French twist. I saw another bruise on her neck and one on her clavicle, probably everywhere, leopard spots of broken veins.

"What have you been up to, Amanda?" I asked. "Where have you been?"

"I'm just being a cat," she said.

"Those are some pretty bad claw marks."

"Let me be a cat, and we'll be just fine. I know how to take care of myself."

I took her hand again and ran my fingers over the marks on it, noting the texture of her skin, smooth as sifted flour. She squeezed my fingers and gently dug her nails into my palm.

"If you're a cat, what does that make me?" I asked.

"You're something, Amit. You really are quite something."

# LITTERMATES

LAUREN AND THE DOG HAD the same dull-blue, wide-set eyes. When I met them at the park by the library, they were also wearing the same shade of bright magenta. This seemed like overkill, so I didn't say anything. Maybe Lauren just liked pink, although she didn't seem like the kind of woman who was into pink, even ironically. She did like irony. That was one of the things we had in common.

The dog was snapped into a pink padded harness, to prevent jumping up. Lauren had long adhesive strips the same color as the harness around one kneecap, from a recent surgery. When she said hello, she made a point of telling me that the surgery was painful and invasive, but she wouldn't take the Vicodin the doctor gave her. The dog lolled at her feet, happy and oblivious.

"What did you do with them?" I asked.

"I flushed them."

"That's terrible for the environment."

She bared her teeth at me. "It's not terrible for my sobriety."

Lauren and I were both in recovery. We have the same sponsor, which makes us littermates. When I was drinking and using, I thought recovery was a big, inclusive club where you go to connect with people and hang out and form lifelong friendships, but, in reality, most of the people I ended up meeting in recovery were kind of shitty. I don't say that to be mean; it's just true.

I'm kind of shitty for saying that, actually. So that's my proof.

I am an alcoholic because I drink myself into the hospital every time I feel like I'm a victim of the future, the *maybe*. The future is a dead lunar surface, empty and open, like a field covered in smooth, silver sand or salt. Fear of the future is why I relapse about every ninety days. That is as long as I can stand to be uncomfortable. I can't accept the future. It is a place where nothing can grow, no matter how much I water it.

Every time I get sober, it's because I hope I have something to look forward to. My sponsor said I was "terminally unique" and she didn't mean it as a compliment, but as a true and accurate statement. I *am* unique. I just don't want to die from it.

*     *     *

THE PUPPY WAS NAMED SAWYER Grey: a big name for a little, wiggly dog. I think the "Grey" was in the name because of the fur color, which was like the color of rain. I scooped it up and snuggled it to my chest. We were sitting in the summer grass at the park, and, if the puppy got away, it'd just fall onto the soft, safe green grass.

"Did you get any callbacks today?" Lauren asked me.

She knew I was looking for a job. Everyone in our recovery group knew, because that's all I talked about in AA meetings—work.

"No. I sent out my resume to a few places."

"Maybe it's a sign," she said, in that way that sober people have that is both irritating and reassuring at the same time. The puppy lunged gently at my face and licked my chin.

"Hey," I said and put it down.

I don't know why I keep saying "it" when the puppy was definitely a girl dog. I guess I don't really believe that everything has a gender, and it feels weird to call a dog "she." It's also weird that people will ask a dog's sex before they greet it. Like, what makes you think the dog cares? Why are you so worried about misgendering a dog?

It's about as weird as calling it a bitch. I'm a feminist but I'm not into reclaiming derogatory words. They feel wrong in my mouth. My own feelings about human genders are complicated, and it just seems unnecessary to slap a gender on every living thing when we can't even accept people's different gender expressions and identities and stuff. I kept thinking, what if the dog was male but still had the pink harness? Would people call it a boy? I was pretty sure I couldn't get past any of my first-visit-only job interviews because I wasn't wearing the right colors for my workplace gender.

Everything about the way I looked and sounded gave me away. I wasn't interviewing because I cared about the job; I was looking for benefits. But you can't say that, even if it's true. *I need insurance so I can be OK in my body for once.*

"Sawyer Grey, come here," Lauren said. She tugged the leash, but not hard. The puppy didn't need that much encouragement; it ran right onto her lap and put its paws on her chest. Lauren was definitely a *she*.

"On the upside, I've gotten really good at filling out applications," I joked.

"I don't even look for work anymore," Lauren said. "It's all referrals at this point. So much easier than knocking on people's doors."

"Yeah," I said. I was thinking about how, if I was a dog trainer, I don't think I would want to give up a puppy I'd named and trained and gotten all ready for its new family. I was also thinking how easy Lauren had it compared to me. She looked like what she was. The people who hired her didn't have to work through awkward feelings regarding their dog trainer. She was someone they felt comfortable paying. She didn't need anything except self-acceptance to feel comfortable in her skin.

Lauren looked at me with her dog eyes, and I knew she was picturing me naked. When your gender is treated like a sideshow act, you get used to being eyeballed. I can feel when people are thinking about what's in my pants. Lauren was more transparent than most.

"Where'd the name come from?" I asked her, just to change the subject.

"Sasha Grey."

"The porn star?"

"I just really like her," Lauren said. "She can take a pounding. It's hot."

I looked down at the grass.

Lauren rubbed Sawyer Grey, who was sitting between her legs. The way her hand moved over the dog's still-stretchy skin made the gesture look obscene.

"You ever think about getting one of these?" she asked me.

"I'm on food stamps and I run out of unemployment next month," I said. "My landlord doesn't allow dogs unless they're service animals. What would I feed a dog?"

"You have plenty of time for one, at least."

"I wish I didn't."

She looked at me through her eyelashes. "I could get you a doctor's note. Sawyer Grey will need a new home in six weeks. I'm training her so she can go to a foster home."

"She's a pit bull."

"I have a certificate that says she's a mastiff mix. Breed banning is immoral. Look at her. Is that the face of a killer?"

The puppy wriggled to its feet. It toddled toward me. Without thinking, I reached out to pat its face. My hand landed in its mouth. I could feel the tiny needles of its future teeth, still latent in its gums. I looked down at my fingers. They tickled the velvet of the dog's tongue. She looked up at me.

"Give that back," I said, and she opened her mouth. My hand wasn't even wet.

"Tell her she's a good girl," Lauren said.

"Good girl," I said to Sawyer Grey, even though it was a total betrayal of my principles. She was a cute puppy. She put her paw on my leg, and her little dewclaw scratched a thin, chalky line on my skin. I licked my finger and rubbed it over the spot, and the pale mark disappeared, turning back into the color of the rest of me.

OUR SECTION OF THE PARK was empty except for some people in matching neon green T-shirts unloading produce crates from a white truck. Across the grass, a few mothers in saris watched their kids play on the metal swings. Lauren and I were doing what unemployed people did at 11:25 a.m. on a Wednesday when everyone else was at work.

Usually at this time I would be heading to one of my recovery meetings to panic about the job offers I wasn't getting. Instead, I was in the park. I rubbed the tips of Sawyer Grey's ears and wondered if dogs got sunburned on days like this. The weather was so hot that, honestly, Lauren and I could have been wearing bathing suits and it wouldn't have been weird.

I will tell you right now that I would never and could never end up with Lauren. She's not butch enough for me, first of all. Also, even though it's super against the rules of AA, our sponsor sometimes tells me the things she and Lauren talk about when they're alone together. These snippets and stories aren't anything bad, exactly, but they are the kind of thing you shouldn't learn from another person.

For example: What if I fell in love with Lauren and we were in bed together and I touched her face while she told me one of the things I've already heard from our sponsor and I had to nod and pretend it was new information and I was a liar who couldn't, like, honor her bravery for revealing herself to me like that? I don't want intimacy that is built on mutual convenience, or that contains a single untruth.

Not that I would ever sleep with someone who was into porn in that way and said things like what she said about Sasha Grey. That's a deal-breaker all by itself. I mean, what if I fell in love with someone who saw all bodies that way, even mine, and that perspective was the thing that kept us from really connecting in a meaningful way? I wouldn't be different to them, I'd be just another piece of flesh to pound. Dog chow. Every time we slept together I would wonder, is this really love or is it just impact?

THE PEOPLE FINISHED UNLOADING THEIR crates, got a big green camping canopy out of the truck, and started to unfold it. I watched how they cooperated with each other. Life was supposed to work like that, with everyone moving in tandem. The canopy had enough shade for all of them, plus a table and two folding chairs. One of the people had a clipboard and nodded at it while the others arranged the crates so that they'd have a cool spot to sit.

I didn't feel secure in God's universe at this moment. I wasn't sure I believed in God, but that didn't really matter because I wasn't that far into the Twelve Steps yet. My unhappiness was sour, pulling on my tongue. I knew that sharing my negativity in meetings, or really anywhere, was stupid: Every time I did, the recovered part of my brain wondered what the fuck did I have to complain about? Here I was, sitting in the sun, sober, with a puppy. But I couldn't get the future off my mind, and it sucked all the color out of the present moment.

"What are you looking at?" Lauren said. She rolled onto her side.

*Her.*

I know what you're thinking. You're thinking that, in this story, I'm going to end up with Lauren even though I already said I wasn't. You're thinking that my self-esteem is so low that I will go to bed with her. I have nothing else to do. My body is the wrong shape from itself. Lauren, to someone like me, is probably looking pretty good. I could use the validation, right?

My sponsor says that being able to read other people's minds only happens in comic books. She'd be angry if I slept with Lauren. The first rule of staying sober is *Don't shit where you eat.* People relapse because they do things they're ashamed of. Or, not exactly ashamed, but not one-hundred-percent comfortable with. It's hard to go to a meeting when you've fucked someone who goes there too. Once you've been naked with someone it's hard to be honest with them, or in front of them, in my experience.

I may like women, but I don't like *all* women.

Besides, I only sleep with people I'm actually already in love with. No one in their right mind has sex just for fun.

The puppy flopped next to Lauren and closed its eyes. Its tongue protruded from its soft lips as though licking the grass. In a moment, it was snoring.

"I'm going to see what they have in those crates," I said and got up as quietly as I could. Lauren turned away from me, leaning over Sawyer Grey like a mother over a snoozing infant.

When I got close to the canopy, I realized that the logos on the volunteers' T-shirts were for a Christian church. The screen print was a cartoon Jesus distributing sardines and baguettes, with a big smile plastered across his face. His toes stuck out of his sandals under his robe. He looked really pumped to be helping people out. This was clearly the artist's interpretation of the loaves and fishes miracle.

I don't think I would look that happy if I was doing a miracle. It probably doesn't feel that great to have divine power channeled through your wimpy human body.

The guy who was holding a clipboard looked me over and smiled, just as big as Jesus. His teeth were crooked: One of the front ones was just a tiny bit longer than its partner, and they folded in together like a collapsing picket fence.

"Would you like something to eat?" he asked. "We have farm-fresh food that needs to go to a good home."

"I'm not Christian," I said.

"Arguably, neither was the Savior," he said. "Can I write your name down, so we know who we've impacted today through our work and faith in the Gospel?"

It didn't look like work to me. Two of the other guys were sharing an energy drink in the shade by the truck. A woman with cockatoo hair sat in a camping chair with her hands folded, as though posing for a photo.

"Hold on," I said. "I didn't say I would take anything."

His smile stiffened for a moment, faster than a microaggression, but I saw it and I knew he was the kind of guy who had to pray in order to tolerate people who were different—like me. He didn't care for people who obstinately resisted the easy categories instead of just going with the program and letting Jesus take the wheel.

I tried hard to imagine Jesus in the farm truck, blasting the new John Mayer album as he delivered fruits and veggies to people in need. But what did I know? People believed all kinds of crazy stuff. For example: I believed that sitting in a church basement and drinking bad coffee with a bunch of drunks would change my life for the better. It worked for ninety days at a time.

I'd always had an issue with needing to belong, though. The best way was to get interested in the things that other people cared about, so in high school I convinced myself that I could stomach alt rock. My need to be liked meant I ended up owning every CD released by The Pixies and other popular bands that the boys I crushed on talked about in the cafeteria. I listened to those albums over and over and read the liner notes as if there was going to be a quiz on the lyrics. Nobody asked me to join in, but I listened. Remembering these things made me squirm inside. I used to be so eager to find common ground with those alien male creatures, to ride in their cars and be pawed by them at football games. Belonging did not come naturally to me, though; that was for people like Lauren, who was born to be the desired one, the girl who knew all the cool songs, who could crack sarcastic jokes without thinking twice, who knew an ollie from a kick flip, and who seemed to have been born with a magical ability to make boys like her and make them think she really liked them back. I had watched girls like that in awe, coming and going in cars that blasted the Pixies or the Smiths; this shared language evaded me. I felt as though I was stranded on an island, all alone with my solitary, quirky brain.

But of all the things I'd tried to make friends, at least I'd never pretended to be interested in Jesus. Not like this guy. He clicked the button on his ballpoint pen.

"You're free to take a look at what we have, sir," he said through gritted teeth.

"Ma'am." I don't even do pronouns, but I couldn't resist.

"Ma'am," he repeated, as a deep, bloody flush crept up his neck and into his cheeks.

Guys like this sent me lewd photos on dating apps and offered to rearrange my guts for me. Christian dads were the worst. No matter how much I learned about their favorite bands or sports teams, or the minutiae of the video games they loved, they never managed to see me as more than a fucktoy. I sympathized with straight women, I really did. They got about ten percent of the harassment I did.

I stepped over to the cockatoo-haired woman, whose smile was so white that it practically made my eyes blister. It was like staring into a supernova.

"Share our bounty," she chirped. She waved toward the crates, which were piled with some fruit I'd never seen. They were the size of a fist, pale yellow, and puckered with prickles.

"Is this cactus?" I asked. I picked one up and was surprised by its heft.

She laughed. I could hear the tolerance. She was doing the Lord's work and wasn't allowed to be rude to me, but underneath I knew she was thinking about Leviticus and about how people like me were an abomination, an insult to God.

"It's a cucumber, a lemon cuke," she said. "Looks like one thing and tastes like something completely different. Appearances can be deceiving. But you always know the tree by its fruit, that's what the Bible says."

"How do you eat it?"

From under the folding table, she produced a knife, which alarmed me. I stepped back out of instinct, with the cucumber still in my hand. She laughed again.

"Jumpy, aren't you."

*You would be too, if you were me.* A couple of women came up, babies on their hips, and started feeling the pile of cucumbers. They wore embroidered scarves to cover their hair. Immaculate athletic trainers poked out from under their dresses. The woman with the knife turned away from me and started talking to the mothers in a loud, clear voice.

"Now, we need your names before you take," she said, nodding rapidly. The guy with the clipboard hovered nearby, waiting to record the good deeds they were performing. They didn't mind people from other countries, but other planets? That was a different issue, I guess.

I backed away and went back to Lauren, who was lying on her back, pointing out the clouds to Sawyer Grey.

"Let's get out of here," I said.

"What was wrong with them?" She rolled toward me.

"They're weirdos. But I got this." I held up the mystery food. "Ever seen one?"

"It's a cucumber," she said, which made me feel like the only person around with a deficient knowledge of exotic produce. Portland was a foodie town, but really, this was too much.

"Some cucumber," I scoffed, but my ignorance was obvious, and she shrugged, like who hasn't seen a lemon cucumber before, were you raised on Pluto or something?

She tugged the dog's leash so it knew we were leaving. The way it looked at Lauren made me feel kind of nauseated, although that could have been the Christians or even just sitting in the sun for too long. Dogs have no discernment. They don't understand what people are really like; they just believe that everyone is going to be kind to them. Must be nice.

Lauren and Sawyer Grey and I walked the long way back around the blooming mock orange bushes. When we got to the big holly hedge that screened the park from the main road, I turned around and waved at the guy with the clipboard. I had the cucumber in my hand. I brandished it like a grenade. It was wonderfully solid, heavy as a small melon. I thought about how good it would feel to throw it back at those people and let it explode on the lawn, split open and seeds everywhere, right in front of them, where everyone could see.

The guy raised his hand, though, and I felt bad, so I didn't do it.

It's negative karma, anyway.

A few blocks into the neighborhood, we found a vacant lot with a chain link fence around it. Huge, thick weeds covered in tiny yellow flowers mingled with grass as high as my knees. The fence was twisted and half torn away from its metal posts, as though someone had yanked and yanked on it, trying to stretch the tension out of the aluminum. It bulged in places, like breasts or a belly. The grass grew through it, unconcerned.

In the center of the lot, two mangy pine trees reached toward each other with bald arms. A squirrel chittered in one of them, and Sawyer Grey lunged through the broken gate, barking and paddling its paws. Lauren tried to get it to heel, but that didn't help, and the dog spun in an agitated circle until the leash was all wrapped around it and it actually fell down with its big dumb puppy feet flailing at the air.

I couldn't help but laugh, which was nice, because Christians give me anxiety. That was the main part of AA that rubbed me wrong: the God talk. Everyone said to just take what I needed and leave the rest, but when you got down to it there wasn't a lot left without God. I encountered a specific flavor of God when I lived down near Ashland and was still trying to fit in with the church community there. I got all tangled up: worse than the dog.

My least favorite feeling is when people sense that you don't belong, or that something is wrong about you, but won't acknowledge their discomfort. They try harder to be friendly and they get extra polite, but they don't know how to treat you because they don't know what the fuck you are. They're not actually welcoming you, after all, they're easing their irritation at having to talk to someone who is difficult, who refuses to be like others. It's worse, in some ways, than a person being straight-up rude, which is horrible but at least it's honest.

Once I knew I was trans and also an alcoholic, I got some labels and some groups to belong to: an identity. I think that helped put people at ease, because instead of getting awkward when I show up or deliberately leaving an empty chair on either side of me, they just say *Hey, Abby*, and it's cool. I don't feel people's eyes on me when I get a second cup of bad coffee, like *Oh, that tranny's stealing from the meeting; they never even put a dollar in the basket and they're taking all the cookies.*

If I could choose a superpower it would definitely not be reading people's minds.

Lauren knelt down and unwound Sawyer Grey. The grass was flattened in one spot, big, as if someone had been making a snow angel in the weeds and pressing them down to make a soft resting place. I saw an orange plastic cap and picked it up, and a couple seconds later I found the syringe that went with it. It was full of black blood, thick and congealed inside the plastic tube. Someone shot up and then pulled the plunger back out as far as it would go.

I capped the needle and threw it over the fence, into the neighbor's bushes. That house was for sale, so nobody would even see it until after the new owners moved in, got around to doing yard work on a sunny day, and found a dirty syringe in their rhododendron.

Lauren was soothing the dog, who was trying to eat the ragweed. I looked again for needles or broken glass, but didn't see any. No cigarette butts, either.

"Come sit over here," I said. "It's nice."

The grass was soft and springy under our bodies. She settled beside me and the dog sprawled across my lap and hers, belly up, gazing at the pines. Lauren stretched her leg out, the one with the pink tape over the knee, and sighed.

"I'm so glad none of this is forever," she said.

I stroked Sawyer Grey's silky head and gently pinched the tips of her ears. She poked her nose into my palm, and I felt her little teeth again, like the points of a dozen pins. I let her work me over with her soft mouth. She was too little not to need some kind of mama. I didn't know where I would be in a couple of weeks, in terms of my recovery or employment or anything else like that, but when I looked at her, I thought maybe I was capable of more than I'd assumed. For once the future didn't feel like an endless, shifting dune.

"I'll take the dog," I said.

"I can get you a doctor's note," Lauren said. "Then she can live with you. And I have her supplies and some food."

I tried imagining it. What if, this time, the story was different? I wondered. The dog liked me, and it wasn't confused by my body or my voice or the other things about me that seemed to repel humans. I'd never had something in my life that wasn't puzzled by me, including myself.

I sniffed the cucumber, explored its hairy nub with the tip of my nose, and bit through its thin, yellow rind. I wasn't expecting it to be so sweet, or its seeds so large, suspended in the pulp like grains of pasta. Lauren took it out of my hand and tasted it too; our bite marks overlapped. She looked at it as though it was a crystal ball that would tell us how the rest of the summer would be.

"I heard these are crossbred between regular cucumbers and sweet oranges, but I think it's just a myth." She let the dog sniff it.

"It's not genetically modified?"

"No. Selective breeding."

She shot me a look of great significance, like *Do you get the message yet?*

I tilted my head back. When you are in recovery, everything is a parable; you are the miracle, peeling back the layers of each epiphany. You are a fable, a moral, or a cautionary tale. Whatever words I chose carried weight, whether I liked it or not, because Lauren was listening and I could tell that the afternoon was already turning into a story for her, something that could be passed along when I was gone and she had traveled past me into the future.

*Abby said she'd take the dog.*

Maybe that was the only thing I could give anyone: a sense that they, at least, were better, cured. That's how stories work. People talk and they make meaning out of happiness or happiness out of meaning. Every little thing is taken, tasted, eaten, shared. So it was written; so shall it be.

# VENUS CONJUNCT SATURN

RIGHT THERE IN ANGIE'S CHART, it said to avoid Scorpios. She was an actual scientist, and so it was clear which side of the "is astrology exact" debate she should have landed on. She knew astrology was a qualitative, atmospheric science, like meteorology—a theory, not a practice. You couldn't use it to reliably predict anything, because its proof was in your lived experience. A horoscope *became* true. But she couldn't seem to keep away.

It didn't matter what the other person's birthday was. Scorpio, didn't matter. Any sign she tried, all of her relationships seemed to be problematic.

Also, there was no such thing as a good, healthy breakup.

Also, being a Pisces, Angie struggled to see problems until they were already right on top of her, rising over her head like a wave that was so big she'd never be able to outswim it. This time, the wave's name was Kate.

She agreed to have an early dinner with Kate even though her personal forecast cautioned against a Venus Conjunct Saturn. She almost never read the planetary movements. The sun sign and sometimes the ascendant were enough to give her an idea of what to expect. Saturn meant conflict, unhappiness, and old wounds. In the conjunct position with Venus, it meant relationship problems. Almost guaranteed. But astrology wasn't *that* accurate—and the more she thought about Kate, the less she wanted to believe in its power to prophesy. Women who made decisions solely based on the positions of the stars or read their daily horoscopes too closely were the objects of derision. She wasn't going to be silly. She closed the horoscope app and texted Kate.

*See you at the gym. I'm gonna earn those happy hour tapas!* She added emojis of a taco and a smiley face. They'd been dating for two months.

Angie packed her gym bag with care, choosing pretty underwear. Sex with Kate was good, even though Angie always wanted the lights off and that was probably going to be a problem at some point. She put in her second favorite bra, along with a blouse that was just the right shade of blue. She was saving up for augmentation, so her Victoria's Secret padded one was doing double duty. She almost never took it off. The hormones she took skewed her body female, so she had a tiny A cup, but not enough for an underwire. Still, a bee sting was a bee sting. Better than nothing.

She didn't have any clean cute workout clothes and had to resort to some old yoga pants and an oversized Olympics '88 Basketball T-shirt. Her trainers were beat up but fine for lifting weights. The gym bag was old, too, from high school. It had Angie's last name embroidered on it, and her varsity letterman pin stuck through the canvas. She traced the gold enamel football with her manicured nail. She'd been the kicker the year they went to State. They won that year, because of her. That was the year people stopped calling her "faggot" and didn't act weird when she changed in the bathroom stall instead of with the guys. One kick. And then, when the transition was over the next semester, she played on the girls' soccer team, and they went to State too.

She liked athletic girls and she liked being an athletic girl. Her body felt right. She ran a lot and did Pilates in her living room. Kate, who was muscular and compact and wore her long black curls in a high ponytail, was completely the kind of girl Angie always fell for. She dated men, sometimes, she told Angie. But it was a Scorpio thing. Kate couldn't help herself. She said that her bisexuality was confusing for everyone except her. She said she wasn't really attracted to people who weren't one or the other. Her eyes were green, with dark lashes. She never said anything about Angie's body, or compared her to other women she'd gone out with. The right moment to tell her the whole story never quite came, so Angie waited, gathering data.

\*     \*     \*

WORK WAS THE LAB WHERE Angie pipetted endless samples of HIV-positive blood into plastic capsules. The building was on a hill in a clinic compound near the Navy hospital. Like every building on the city's west side, it had a slice of view: the river, dotted with white boats and sometimes teams of people rowing in the wake behind them. The blue seemed small and far away to Angie; the buildings on the east bank were indistinguishable from one another. Her lab was on the fourth floor and looked over the parking lot, the security fence, condos and houses, and the tiny strip of marina. The view was more sky than water from up here. Honestly, it was a nice distraction from both the blood and Angie's squirmy feelings about Kate, who was probably jogging in slow motion on the waterfront Angie could almost see from here. It wasn't difficult to imagine Kate in a crop top and shorts, tanned and soaked in just the right amount of sweat. She wasn't a cheater, she told Angie, right from the start. She couldn't help it that people were attracted to her. The thing with Scorpios is: They are irresistible and they know it. They have that look to them. And even early on, Angie was super-attracted to Kate, so this was proof that it must be true.

Relationships are an imprecise science.

They weren't going to cure AIDS, at least not today. That's what the sign in the lab said, in the director's neat block letters. It was about data, not miracles. Most of the blood was from primates who'd been infected by the virus. That's what the security fence was for—to keep out animal rights activists. Angie wasn't sure how, but PETA had found out where the samples came from and now the lab got bomb threats. After the last one, the director told everyone to start parking behind the main building, out of sight from the perimeter. He was worried that the activists might target someone individually, follow their car home or track their license plate. Nobody told Angie that lab research would be so risky when she was still in school. She had a Greenpeace bumper sticker and another one that said *Love Our Mother*. She didn't see anything wrong with using monkey blood.

*   *   *

QUALITIES OF THE PISCES SUN sign, besides having trouble saying "no" to people who weren't good for her, included: loves the color blue; is naturally emotional, sympathetic, secretive, and difficult to read; has psychic powers; and is happiest when near the water. Angie believed all these things about herself, because they kept turning out to be true. If her lived experience was the research, she had enough data to confirm that, yes, being born in early March resulted in certain personal qualities she couldn't seem to shake. One day, the app suggested trying to actively manifest her Pisces energy, so she taped a postcard on her work bench's black, industrial-grade-steel panel. It showed an image of a salmon frantically leaping against the current of a waterfall. The salmon was pink and green and reminded Angie of the wetsuits surfers wore.

"Spawn 'til you die, huh?" said Brandon, Angie's bench partner. He tapped the glossy picture. "You ever seen these things in the wild? They swim until their flesh falls off."

"Sexy," said Angie. She imagined the smell: a river full of rotting, writhing salmon.

"I'm like, damn. Splash it up my back, daddy. It's like Fire Island for fish."

It probably wasn't a coincidence that the only two queer people were at the same bench. Angie didn't mind, because she liked Brandon. Brandon didn't mind, because it meant he could be as salty as he wanted.

On their first day, Brandon joked, "What am I going to do, pretend to be straight? Let me tell you about the last time I faked something for eight hours." His eyes met Angie's. *Are you offended? Am I too much?*

"Eight hours? That's how long it took my last date to propose," Angie said.

His laugh was quick, relieved. So they were allowed to be like this with each other.

"But seriously, Angie. What's with the fish?"

"I just like it."

He looked at her, arched an eyebrow. She could practically hear the double entendres. But then he shook his head. "Well, I'm sticking with primates. Did you hear that we got another grant for this quarter?"

"Nobody told me."

"I made a new friend in the accounting office," he said. "Still working on getting that raise."

"Get it, girl," Angie said.

"Girl. It's been got."

They unloaded the box of blood bags and started the process of siphoning each one into a series of sterile containers. Each pint had to be divided into individual bubbles, sterile plastic test tubes of half a fluid ounce each. The blood was dark and richly purple. High in iron, Angie thought, plunging a needle through the bag's double plastic membrane. She wondered what they fed the monkeys to enrich their blood like this. A small amount of anticoagulant was added to each pint, but it had no effect on the lab's tests.

After this, the blood would be agitated for a specific amount of time to separate the hemoglobin. There were washes. There were slides and solutions. They were looking for a vaccine for HIV, a new preventative that would keep the virus from appropriating the CD4 helper lymphocyte cells. The research program was essential to the vaccine; a miracle drug could save millions of lives. *Isn't that worth a few monkeys?* A world where children knew their grandparents, where a common cold wasn't a death sentence was possible, one pipette of primate hemoglobin at a time.

"What are you doing tonight?" Brandon asked. "Fly-fishing?"

"I'm going out with Kate. It's make-or-break time."

"Oh, shit." He side-eyed her but didn't stop squeezing the pipette. "Is that normal?"

"I really like her. It's weird, though—I can't read her. Like, I don't feel like I can be completely truthful with her."

"So, this is, like, commitment?"

"It's been two months." And before he could say it for her, she added: "That's like eight years in lesbian time. We're either getting married at this point or we're dead."

Brandon nodded, pushed the wire rack of samples aside, and picked up a new box. He turned it over in his hands as if inspecting a present. Angie heard the new plastic tubes inside rattling against one another. Maybe it wasn't that she wanted to break things off with Kate; she just didn't know enough to decide if she wanted to keep going. And Kate, after all, knew practically nothing about Angie.

"Why can't you be honest?" Brandon asked.

"Let's just say that it's never worked in my favor." She looked at Brandon very hard, beaming her private history at him. The year of injections, the bottom surgery, the first time wearing mascara to school, the first girl she kissed who didn't see her as anything other than a "she." The pleasure of not having a complicated story to tell when she moved to Portland. Of not being misgendered, ever. Of leaving the transition behind and just being *Angie*. The relationships that had lasted two months apiece, exactly, and the painful periods of self-doubt in between. The Pisces sign that shimmered over all of it, making it impossible for Angie to stick to anything with anyone.

"Do you know what I mean?"

Brandon blinked. "I'm just glad you're not a straight woman," he said. "Propping up a hetero ego is exhausting."

Angie laughed and turned back to her pipette. "I'm definitely not straight."

"You are what you say you are," Brandon said. "If Kate can't handle that, or if she doesn't believe you, well, then she doesn't deserve you."

"Thanks."

"That's common sense, not a pep talk."

"Absolutely. One hundred percent pep-free."

She knew she'd try to tell Kate tonight and have faith that maybe, this time, she wouldn't feel horribly ashamed or exposed. Maybe Kate wouldn't sit there and say hateful, transphobic things, or make Angie feel like a fraud or like she should apologize for the way she lived, or degrade Angie, or make cruel comments about Angie's appearance, about *passing* or the way Angie liked to have sex, which as far as she could tell wasn't that different from the way cisgendered lesbians liked to have sex, because after all weren't those the women she was sleeping with? The ones who were so proud of their gold stars and their No Dicks Allowed girls-only-camp status symbols, even though it was stupid to define yourself by what you *wouldn't* fuck. Angie was just as much a woman as any of them and should probably have her own gold star because she'd never been with a man either, and wasn't interested, and deeply resented being told, as one particularly nasty girl had said to her after a few drinks when Angie got up the courage to mention the transition, that *If you ever had a dick then you're never going to be one of us* and then she said that Angie was a secret gold star stealer, which was a shitty thing to say plus untrue, and the evening ended in tears. Angie was so sad and hungover the next day that she couldn't even go to work and feel like at least Brandon appreciated her. But they worked together. And he was a Gemini. The friendship had its own subtle borders, and she knew better than to lean on him any harder than she already did.

At five p.m., she got her gym bag and went to change in the employee washroom.

"Good luck," he said as she passed him.

"Thanks, Bee."

SHE AVOIDED LOOKING AT HERSELF in her gym clothes and was glad that the washroom didn't have a full-length mirror. Going to the gym as a date wasn't the usual for her, especially in non-cute clothes that didn't immediately signal *femme*. When Angie walked into the boxing gym,

Kate was already there, warming up with a jump rope. Heavy metal was pumping out of a stereo in the corner; the roll-up doors were open to let some of the noise and heat out, make the place less claustrophobic. It wasn't just the music: The place stank like men and musk and sweat. Kate went every day. She was a competitive MMA fighter, so if she wasn't doing push-ups or punching a weighted bag, she was running sprints and talking strategy with her coach. One time, Angie asked her if she liked it, and she said it's what she was good at.

"It's a mixed blessing, though. Because once someone finds out you're a boxer, all they want to do is hit you."

Angie dropped her bag near the bank of lockers and wandered over to the squat cage. It had been a long time since she'd lifted like this— Pisces, mostly water, preferred cool and dark places. She was already sweating, and her hair stuck to the back of her neck. Her shirt was going to get wrecked.

"Hey," Kate panted. "You want help with that rack?"

"Is that a line?"

"No, cutie. Just wondered if you wanted a spot."

"I'm good."

And like magic, Angie felt the old armor grow over her, the way she used to feel leaving the locker room for a game, walking into a stadium with hundreds of people all pointing their voices at her. She shouldered the bar, lifted it out of its brackets, and dropped down until her thighs were parallel to the floor. Popped back up. *One.* Lowered down. Pop. *Two.* Three sets of fifteen reps later, her legs felt nice, like taffy. She pulled the plates off the bar, just to be polite, and neatly stacked them where she'd found them.

"Coach wants me doing more cardio," Kate said. She was resting between sets of sit-ups on a reverse incline bench. Angie slipped her hands over Kate's feet. Were they girlfriends? Did they look like girlfriends? They were the only women in the gym.

"I only run when I'm late for the bus."

Kate grinned. "Liar. You drive everywhere."

"For real. I haven't done heavy weights in a decade, just yoga and stuff. I'm surprised my form hasn't broken down."

"You lifted?"

"For football. And then soccer. High school and college."

Kate leaned back and folded her hands behind her head. "You had an all-girl football team in high school? That's progressive."

Then she was in the set, no talking. So Angie didn't have to answer. She felt her sign's scales clicking around her, protecting her. Here, in a boxing gym in the city, she was only what she seemed to be. Her real self was alive only in the present moment. *You are what you say you are.*

THE SECOND PART OF THEIR date was Angie worrying about what exactly she was supposed to say. She was afraid to wait any longer than two months. She'd determined that it was actually the perfect length of time for this kind of talk. Any longer and it would seem she was concealing something. Any sooner and the person she was dating might not have the time to develop a connection to her without that label in the way. She didn't believe in labels; she believed in astrology, because it was more useful and more meaningful. It helped people. As she followed Kate into the restaurant, she analyzed a series of possible outcomes.

Kate wore a dress the color of monkey blood. She slid onto a seat at the bar, and the bartender came over with a dish of Thai cashews and the list of small plates. Angie took the stool next to her, sitting close enough that their arms touched. They ordered off the same laminated card. When their drinks came—a rosé, a sweet mojito—they traded sips, getting lipstick on each other's glasses.

"We're so gross," Kate said. "I would be sicked out by us, if I wasn't so happy."

Angie eyed their reflection in the mirror over the bar. "We're pretty."

"I'm just here to plant the seed of envy in other bitches' hearts," Kate said dramatically. She flicked her hair over her shoulder.

"It's working for you," Angie said. She nibbled the lime wedge from her drink. "I'm happy too. I can't believe it's been two months."

"Two moons."

"What's your favorite thing about us?" Angie asked. *Please don't say our honesty.*

Kate smiled at her in the mirror. She'd lined her top and bottom lashes and her eyes were huge, delicate as moths. "Do I have to pick a favorite? Okay, I'll play. I like that you're patient with me."

"Nobody's ever described me as patient."

"But you are," Kate said. "I love that we've been seeing each other for two months and I feel like you just take your time with me. You don't try to get me to change. You're not texting me all the time."

Maybe they weren't girlfriends, if that's what normal girlfriends did. Angie mentally reviewed her texting frequency: usually once or twice a day, something cute or funny. Should she have been trying to see more of Kate? Was her interest not clear enough?

Kate went on about her need for independence and her busy schedule, and Angie's heart started to ache in her chest. Maybe this was breakup talk, which she wasn't prepared for since she'd been so focused on Kate's potential rejection of her physical history, and in true Pisces fashion she had gotten lost in the current of those thoughts and totally forgotten that Kate's version of the relationship, if that's even what they were doing, might be different or even in conflict with her own.

She tried to focus on Kate's words, but everything felt slippery and strange. She could sense Venus rising over them, luring her out of hiding. She regretted saying yes to a date. She should have listened to her horoscope and stayed away from Kate and the feelings that Kate evoked in her. In an hour, Venus would position itself over her, and then what? It was supposed to be the planet of romance, but Angie felt its influence piercing her, forcibly peeling back the many protective layers she'd constructed around herself. It hurt. Vulnerability comes from *vulnus*: a wound. A fish with bloody gills.

She took shallow breaths through her mouth and tried to listen to Kate, who kept talking as though nothing was wrong.

"I'm just intrigued by you," Kate was saying. "Usually I get bored so quickly. People get all up in my life, try to tell me all about themselves. You're different."

"I am?"

"It's great," Kate said, and leaned over, and her cheek was by Angie's. "You're great," she said in Angie's ear.

She stroked the goosebumps on Angie's arm.

"You," Angie said, but she was smiling, and Kate was a Scorpio, the unstoppable sign of sex, and she knew *exactly* what she was doing. Their fingers interlaced on the bar.

"The other thing I like is that you don't have to explain everything. Or make yourself more interesting. Ever had that happen? With my ex, sometimes, it was like she was reading me a user manual. All those bells and whistles. Features included in this relationship."

"How long did you date her?"

"Long enough to figure out that I don't want bells and whistles."

Angie smiled. "What do you want?"

"I want to take our time. I want all your time and I want to take it slow."

What that was code for, Angie wasn't sure, but later, in Kate's bed, Kate showed her that *slow* did not mean a chaste or restrained knowledge of the body. She lifted Angie's skirt and put her mouth on her and then kissed her and then put her mouth down there again, back and forth with Angie's hands in her hair, unsure of whether to pull or push because it felt so good. Sheets the color of hemoglobin too. Even though they had the light on, too, for a change, Kate lit a row of candles by the bed. They left sultry trails of wax on their metal stand that dripped down toward the carpet. Kate dropped the spent match into the wastepaper basket and knelt by Angie.

"What's this?" she said. She traced one of the flat, white, soft scars on Angie's labia.

Angie sat up, propped on her elbows. Her legs were open. She looked down at Kate, who rested between them. "Surgery scars."

Kate looked at her. Her fingers moved over the skin, gently, feeling the length of the incision. "Does this hurt?" she asked.

"No."

"I'm not your first?"

"No."

"You're mine."

Her body covered Angie's like a wave, and their limbs mingled, pressing so closely that soon even their skin was the same temperature. Angie's lover moved against her, rocking them both, until Angie could feel Venus in transit above them. This time, she didn't try to slip away. She let the bright star pull her up from this body she loved, her beautiful body with its quirks and depths. As she and Kate flared up together, the sheepskin rug began to smoke, but she couldn't stop, couldn't think, couldn't even be afraid. She felt herself bursting open. She began to cry out. It felt so good, to trade who she'd pretended to be for someone who was loved, universally, and the blaze was brighter and brighter until she could hold nothing back, and its heat held all of her and Kate, illuminating every tender place.

# REDHEAD

LISA LOVED TENNESSEE WILLIAMS UNTIL she had to teach him. Watching a dozen bad Blanche DuBois monologues made her want to hit herself in the head with a goddamn hammer. Conflating volume with emotion, her students dialed up the drama. The high, creaking notes that they injected into their stage voices irritated her. They couldn't project. They forgot their lines. Most of them had never even heard a real Southern accent and sounded as if they were auditioning for *The Beverly Hillbillies*.

"He was a boy, just a boy, when I was a very young girl," twelve times in a row. Over and over. Each one trying to outdo the others for *gravitas*. None of them seemed to grasp the revelation at the center of the monologue. Lisa wanted to scream, *He killed himself because he was gay!* But the magnitude of that didn't register. They'd never heard of Matthew Shepard. Gay marriage was legal. Ellen DeGeneres was out. Nobody seemed to care about queerness in this generation. It didn't mean anything to them.

By the end of workshop, Lisa was brutally frustrated and couldn't stand to go straight home. The students clustered into little groups, giving each other critiques. Instead of staying to talk, Lisa headed for a quiet restaurant a block from her apartment. Class had destroyed what little concentration she had (that was the thing about students; they took up all her energy) and she needed someplace quiet to sit, offstage.

She sat at the counter and took the laminated happy hour menu from between the salt and pepper shakers. She read the cocktail list, knowing she wouldn't order anything from it. She knew enough not to be an actress who drank; it never ended well. She was better off picking at a dish of cashews while the dishwasher told jokes with the cook over the divider between the bar and the kitchen. After a while, the server put a Diet Coke in front of her.

She looked at the traffic, the cars with cloudy windows and buses passing at twenty-minute intervals. Portland was a perfect setting for a play, because it was a place where nothing ever seemed to happen. Within its static, lovely landscape were quiet spots to sit, protected from the noise and opinions of other people. It was a good place for someone who was tired of being looked at.

The bar had a television, of course—relatively small and discreet. They were everywhere these days. The screen showed men in felt hats dragging an iron statue off its pedestal. Lisa shook her head. Show business was politics, and politics was show business.

The server changed the channel, settling on a nature program. A mother whale and her calf nuzzled one another in Hawaii's blue, bath-temperature waters.

"Soup," the server said. "Future soup."

"What?"

"In Japan. They hunt whales."

"I thought it was just sharks," Lisa said.

"Nobody is out there trying to save the sharks."

She shrugged. "I guess."

"You vegan?"

"No."

"Don't start. It's a slippery slope. Next thing you know, you're allergic to gluten and wondering why your acupuncturist won't return your calls."

She laughed. "You speak from experience?"

He crossed his arms and frowned at the whales on TV. "You know how big that baby is? The size of a school bus, at least."

"If only they had a way of defending themselves," Lisa said. His patter was good, better than most of her students'. Or maybe her end-of-day fatigue was lowering her standards; her voice felt lazy and thick.

"It doesn't pay to taste good," the server said. Shaking his head, he went into the kitchen.

A woman in a red wool coat walked past the windows, paused in the doorway, and shook her umbrella. Lisa glanced at her, then turned abruptly away. Shana was the only other new hire, still untenured. She and Lisa had started at the same time—mercifully, not in the same department. Shana taught a class on women's political history, plus a French class five days a week. She insisted on teaching Cixous and Irigaray in the original, even at a state university. Her shoes and clothes were conspicuously expensive. She had strawberry blonde curls that grew like bed springs from her head. She lacked screen appeal. Her eyes searched the corners of a room, ratlike, before coming to rest on what was right in front of her.

Shana, meeting Lisa, had said that *she'd* been an actress too. She'd had a bit part in a raunchy comedy flick. The role recurred in the TV spin-off's pilot but was so small that it was written out of the first season. She hadn't done anything after that. She "wasn't moved to try the stage," she said, which was "all Portland really offered." Which was a way of not saying *I failed at acting*.

"Is that you?" she asked now, sliding onto the stool next to Lisa. "I thought so."

Lisa took a preparatory swallow of her soda. "I was just leaving."

"Oh, stay. Just for a few minutes. I'm sure we'll find something to talk about."

Lisa sighed. She had noticed that Shana, like God, worked in a series of unlikely coincidences, always coming closer than she was wanted.

"Actually, I do have to go—I've got a meeting."

"With whom?" Shana's eyes snapped onto Lisa's face, watching for any twitch, any hint of discomfort.

Lisa was mystified by Shana's competitiveness. Lisa had experienced this kind of jealous bullying and measuring-up when she worked in L.A. She didn't understand the point of it, so she did what she'd always done and simply detached. All semester, she'd just floated away when Shana took a pointed interest in the number of classes Lisa taught, how many students attended and how much they liked her, her upbringing and where she had gone to school, her merits as an academic, where her papers were published (online or in print), and her successes (romantic or professional). Lisa kept her at arm's length, listening but not hearing what Shana had to say.

"The head of something. I don't remember," she lied. She didn't have any such meeting, but Shana didn't need to know that.

"I'm sure it'll be fine," Shana said. She smiled, as though to be conciliatory. "You don't have anything to worry about, do you?"

Lisa finished her Coke much faster than she would have liked and stood to go. "I wish I could stay longer," she said.

"Always nice to catch up," said her rival. "Do you have my phone number? We should get coffee soon. Something less impromptu."

"I have it," Lisa lied as she darted for the door. "Don't forget your umbrella."

But she was angry, walking home—at feeling discovered and by someone she avoided as much as possible. The unspoken rule was, if you were both queer, you had to be friends or like each other. But that was another thing that had changed with mainstream acceptance, Lisa thought. It wasn't a big deal to be gay anymore, and that meant we didn't have to stick together the way we used to. Assimilation took away the fun of playing *us versus the straights*. Community was something that only happened at dance clubs, Madonna concerts, and the annual AIDS walk. That kind of togetherness was a holdover from the eighties in every way. Shana repelled her. As far as Lisa could tell, Shana was incapable of making or maintaining friendships with other lesbians.

Lisa went home and managed to get her brother on the phone at their usual time. He was in rehab again, so she cheered him up by pretending to be Judy Garland, Kermit the Frog, or Ronald Reagan. He adored her voices and sometimes made requests: *Do Marilyn Monroe piloting a 747. Do Mel Gibson, sharing at an AA meeting.* She loved making him laugh; it was about the only thing she felt good about today.

They talked on the phone for half an hour, all the time he was allowed. She pretended to be a Scottish weatherman, forecasting snow in Tahiti that looked like wee sheep sprinkling from heaven. Jeremy gasped for air.

"I'm going to pee," he hiccupped.

"I don't see golden showers on the radar," Lisa said in her bad Sean Connery accent, and her brother almost dropped the phone, he was laughing so hard.

She didn't tell people her brother was a heroin addict anymore. She'd brought it up in a technique class once, and one of the other students had said, *Wow, I'm jealous; you'll always have something tragic to work with.* In L.A., that was the only reason to care about the people in your life. They became your motivation while you tried to make your lines feel real.

A FEW DAYS LATER, JUST as she passed the oversized plaque with Portland State's name on it, Lisa saw a flash of cardinal out of the corner of her eye. She barely had time to blink before Shana slipped in beside her: a sneak attack.

"Going to class? I don't know how you survive without an umbrella," Shana said. Hers covered herself and Lisa as well. Lisa found herself immediately missing the feeling of rain on her coat. Shana's voice drowned out the rain's intimate patter with its nasal dullness. Lisa had to concentrate to catch Shana's words; she hadn't had enough coffee for this.

Shana went on, rapid-fire, without waiting for a response. "Not sure if you heard, but my department is sponsoring a gala on campus. It's a Women's March fundraiser with some amazing speakers. Angelina Jolie is doing the keynote. I got you a ticket, so we can go together. I wanted to tell you yesterday, but you weren't at your office hours."

Lisa didn't tell Shana that she'd met Angelina before, and Uma and Meryl too, ages ago, on a job in Los Angeles. She avoided the implicit comparison: They were *real* actresses. She didn't measure up to Shana's idea of what a performer should look like. Lisa didn't do wardrobe. Lisa was never *in character*, while Shana was always performing.

She said, "I had a migraine and had to go home."

"You get a lot of those; have you gotten it checked? I hope you'll have a makeup time, if you haven't already. Our department has had some really strict crackdowns on adjuncts who come up short on their term requirements. It would be awful to lose your fellowship because you had a little headache."

"Migraine."

"I've never had one. It's mind over matter to me." She flashed a big smile at Lisa. She was close enough that Lisa could have seized her lower lip in her teeth and yanked her greasy grin right off her face.

"Feminism is very *au courant.* It's a provocative topic. You can come to the event, right? I put you on the guest list, so please don't make me regret it."

"I'm not really up on current affairs," Lisa said.

"It doesn't matter how current you are. I just don't want you coming down with some affliction at the last minute. It's a very exclusive list. They couldn't even announce the time and location until this morning because of security issues."

Lisa sighed. This was not an invitation; it was a summons. Shana would not take no for an answer, had made it impossible to do anything except comply.

"Of course I'll come."

"Oh, good. There's a reception after. I'm wearing red, since that's my signature color. Everyone will be wearing something professional looking, so I think I'll go vintage. You can wear black or dark purple and you should probably try to be at least a little sexy. You know, to make up for how you dress during the week."

"What do you mean?"

"Well, just *look* at you."

Lisa looked down at herself. She was wearing brown corduroys, her favorite red shoes, a blue blouse with tiny anchor shaped buttons, a light blue cardigan, and her oversized black raincoat. Her hair was messy, the way she liked it, and, aside from her customary dab of lip balm, her face was bare. She felt naked, exposed. She looked like what she was: a gay acting teacher in her late twenties, a blank screen ready for projection.

Shana's idea of whom she should pretend to be made her furious. Who was she, to decide Lisa's role like that? Lisa was not going to put up with it. This was the other thing about being the only other lesbian on campus, you ended up making concessions to another woman that you would never, ever make to a man. If Shana had been male, Lisa would have reported him. But she was *community*, which made Lisa feel trapped and frustrated. She could never say no, because Shana was always right there. This fact made Lisa so angry that she had to pause outside her classroom door to wipe the anger off her face. When she walked in, she was composed again, ready to act her part. She impersonated a theater professor who still loved Tennessee Williams. Her itchy feeling began to melt away.

"Williams compares Blanche to a moth or uses candlelight and lanterns to suggest her fragility," she explained. "Onstage, you are using the same gestures you perform when you're sleeping, eating, or doing anything that feels 'natural' to you—but you're doing it deliberately. This code is embedded in every action and inaction of yours in a performance. The audience can see it. They're looking for it. Every word that you speak reveals your character, even as your mimicry reinforces the separation between these behaviors and your true, original self."

They talked about staging and did a few passes on the monologue again, this time adding props. Everyone had an easier time when they had an object in their hands, something to play with that linked them to the real world. Maybe they got it. Lisa felt better when class was over.

She straightened her shirt and pulled up her rain hood as she went back out into the weather. Yes. Two could play at this. She would wear blue tonight and she would take Shana off guard.

*    *    *

Lisa's last red carpet had been just before she applied to teach at Portland State. She worked on a big budget film, a spy flick with a superstar cast. In the key scene, Channing Tatum rescued Elizabeth Olsen from an iceberg loaded with explosives. Lisa's job had been doubling for Elizabeth in lighting tests and costume fittings, which meant long hours in a harness, hanging from various high places and being sprayed with fake rain. The film featured an ocean liner, heavy special effects for waves and snow, a speed-boat chase scene, and an extended shootout with the villain, played by Gary Oldman. Because it also included cameos by half a dozen A-list stars, the carpet was packed with people and paparazzi. Lisa's invitation was a courtesy, an acknowledgment of the time she'd put in on the set and her support of the picture's female lead. Elizabeth had already requested her for her next role, which was in a superhero film, the first in a series. Doubling was a great opportunity, Lisa knew, especially for someone who loved to act but didn't covet the limelight. She asked her brother, who was newly sober again, to be her date.

He was supposed to pick her up at four, so they could have "old people dinner," as he called it. Elizabeth kindly lent Lisa one of her formal dresses, since they had the same measurements, and Lisa zipped herself into it and waited for her brother to arrive. At half-past four, he texted that something had come up and he'd meet her at the theater, but didn't respond when she called him to ask what was going on. She felt the first tingle of panic.

She caught a cab across town and walked a whole block in her silk stilettos, past the crowd of fans and photographers popping shots of the celebrities as they arrived. The noise was unbelievable. Lisa's borrowed dress was a doll-pink crepe wool, and she was conscious of how much she was sweating and how she was walking too fast for a dress cut like this. When she got to the front of the theater, she was panting. Someone took a photo of her, mistaking her for someone who was *somebody*: she had the right coloring, the right body type, the right dress and hair and makeup. She was nobody, though.

The red carpet was lined with screaming people. The sound of their voices filled Lisa's ears and made her feel disoriented, though she knew it was just adrenaline, and that this was normal for everyone, especially in L.A. She looked around for Jeremy, who'd stopped responding to her frantic texts, and realized that she wouldn't find him here. He wasn't coming.

He'd relapsed. She felt it. Maybe—overdosed again.

She stood under the theater marquee long enough for a security guard to come over and ask to see her invitation, which she shoved into his hand before she bolted back toward the curb, frantically waving at the passing taxis. The mass of people parted as she wedged herself through them. The borrowed dress snagged. She felt it tear. Then she got into a cab, and the nightmare of dealing with her brother's addiction started all over again.

The movie got terrible reviews, but was a hit at the box office, especially in the Asian and overseas markets. The release date fell on a slow week in August; people just wanted something mindless to watch. Lisa never saw it. She sent Elizabeth a message thanking her but said a family emergency had come up and she'd had to change her plans at the last minute. Elizabeth was gracious, of course. *Keep the dress; I never wear it*, she'd said. *Take care.*

PINK WOOL WAS WRONG FOR a women's rights gala. In a boutique dressing room, Lisa tried on one thing after another. She appraised her reflection. She cleaned up just fine.

The saleswoman knocked on the door: "Is there anything else? How does everything fit?"

Lisa peered over the door and said, "I think we're getting close."

The saleswoman nodded. "Don't take this the wrong way, but I feel like I know you," she said. "Have we met before? You seem so familiar."

Her voice, her face. She was a little piece of every actress she'd doubled for. She could have stayed in L.A., working with Elizabeth and following her from project to project. It was better money than teaching, but Portland had better treatment centers and that's what Jeremy needed.

"I get that a lot," was all she said.

Dress, eyebrow pencil, legs shaved smooth, powder, scent, the arranging of her hair. She painted her face in the bathroom mirror, which lost its layer of steam as she worked and thus slowly revealed to her the crisp outline of her true appearance.

She sat on the edge of her bed and carefully rolled stockings over her legs, then took her new dress off its hanger, undid the long zipper, and stepped into it so she wouldn't stain it with her painted face. She was able, with some contortion, to do it up by herself, and then she slipped her feet into the black high heels she'd worn exactly twice. She smoothed the front of the dress with her hands; the satin caressed her palms. She felt delicious. She went down the hallway to the stairs enveloped in gorgeousness. She could not wait to arrive and really show herself off.

THE EVENT WAS INSIDE A campus lecture hall, with armed security at every one of the doors. They checked her purse, patted her body, and inspected her ID. Then they directed her to a queue of formally dressed people who were waiting their turn to walk through a metal detector. She got through, and, as she picked up her bag, her phone started to ring. She assumed it was Shana, with some last-minute instructions, but she fished it out anyway. The number wasn't one she recognized. She answered.

As soon as she said hello, one of the security team took the phone out of her hand, ended the call, and powered off the phone.

"I'm sorry," he said. "We can't allow electronics or recording devices of any kind at this event. For everyone's safety. You need to leave your phone at the coat check."

"But what if that was an emergency?" Lisa sputtered.

"Do you know what people can do with a mobile phone? This is a detonator," he lectured, handing it back to her. "A radio. It's not safe. And whatever is said tonight doesn't need to make its way to the Internet. We have instructions for a total blackout. No photos, no audio, no video. If you need to make a call, you will have to leave the building. You will not be readmitted. Coat check will give you a tag, so you can get your belongings back after the event."

She nodded.

He smiled and turned back to the line of people by the metal detector.

"Thrilling, isn't it?" said a familiar voice. Shana was at her elbow, materializing as she always did like a demon in a morality play.

"Where did you come from?" Lisa asked.

Shana ignored her. "Angelina is in our row," she said. "She's *so* thin. And shorter than I thought. Actresses are always a lot smaller than they look onscreen. When I was in that film, I was the tallest woman on set. Gigantic."

*Film*, even though it was a throwaway, straight-to-video comedy. Lisa tried not to roll her eyes. Shana was right, though: Angelina was thinner than the last time Lisa had seen her. She sat in the center of the front row with an empty chair on either side of her. She was reading. When Shana stood in front of her, she looked up, those famous lips parting in a polite smile.

"It is so great to meet you," Shana said. She stuck her hand out.

Angelina did not close her book. She took Shana's fingers and gently squeezed them in the gesture of a queen acknowledging some lesser person. Shana beamed. She opened her mouth, but Lisa, who recognized when a star wanted to be left alone, grabbed her by the elbow.

"Let's find our seats," she said.

Angelina's eyes flicked over her face. "You worked with Liz," she said. Her smile was genuine this time, and its warmth felt like an embrace to Lisa. That was star power: When they acknowledged you, you felt really *seen*. The feeling was addictive. People loved it, and couldn't help but want more; they would spend hundreds of dollars a year to see pictures of that smile. A billion-dollar industry was built around the simple desire to be in this woman's presence.

"Last year," Lisa said. "She's terrific."

"She really is," Angelina said. "She's coproducing my next project."

Which, in the language of L.A., meant that Lisa was favored because she was included in this knowledge. Her association with another star meant she could be trusted.

"I can't wait to see it," Lisa said. She received another golden smile, which tingled through her body. How could she ever have left this other world, with these beautiful, wonderful beings in it? She took Shana's arm and steered her away.

Their seats were at the far end of the row, at an awkward angle to the stage. Shana insisted on sitting where she could see Angelina and the other notables. She fluffed her hair and swiveled her head, obviously trying to catch a glimpse of someone worth seeing.

"You didn't tell me you *knew* her," she snarked.

Lisa shrugged. "I don't. Besides, there is no reason she'd think of me. L.A. is a big town. Once you're gone, people tend to let you go."

"You should have asked her to meet us at the reception."

It was useless to explain what a gross violation of Angelina's time that would be, so Lisa just smiled and opened her program. The theater filled, and soon she was surrounded by people and their quiet chatter, laughter, and rustlings—audience noise. She felt the tiny rush it created. The familiar, glorious feeling she always got before a show came back. She closed her eyes and let it wash over her. For a moment, time stopped, reversed, changed shape, and curled on itself, purring.

Then she felt a cold hand on her knee. She opened her eyes, but the lights were dimmed. Shana was stroking her leg with icy fingers, working under the hem of Lisa's dress.

"You never look this pretty," she whispered in Lisa's ear. "I see why Angelina remembered you."

Lisa's hand slapped down, pinning Shana's. "Stop," she said.

"I bet you're good at being quiet," Shana said, and Lisa leaned away as Shana's teeth, along with that lipstick that she hated and the perfume that stank because it was Shana's signature musk, came close to Lisa's ear.

"I'll scream."

"You will when I make you," Shana said. Lisa wriggled away from her and stood, even though the applause was surging and the first pair of security guards was coming from the wings to flank the stage. Shana stood, too, and so did everyone else. A deafening ovation flooded the theater.

Shana's mouth was moving, but Lisa turned away and ran up the aisle toward the exit. The guard at the door let her through, and she went straight into the lobby and pounded on the desk of the vacant coat check window.

"Can I get some help," she said.

Another guard in a severe black suit got up from her stool and put her phone in her pocket. "Sorry," she said. "I thought it wasn't over yet."

"Hasn't even started," Lisa said. She shoved her ticket at the woman and waited impatiently for her to get the plastic bin of phones, each one labeled with a numbered, pink Post-It note. She expected to hear Shana's shoes clacking toward her at any moment. The guard handed back her device, and Lisa snatched it, said thank you, and darted for the main doors. She didn't care if she couldn't come back. She should have known, suspected. She wiped her dress off, trying to get rid of the sensation of Shana's fingers and the sultry, sticky smell that stayed with her even when she headed through the Park Blocks. Her hands were shaking, but she had her phone, so she felt safe. Even though she had no one to call for help, it made her feel that maybe, if she needed it, she could.

She had two missed calls, both from the same number.

"Hey, sis," Jeremy said. "I checked myself out. I'm going downtown right now. I don't have a place lined up and I know this is short notice, but I was hoping I could crash with you. Everything is fine. Call me back."

The other message was from one of the counselors at his rehab: They'd found a small, empty vial in Jeremy's bed. He denied the vial was his, said it was a plant, and walked out when the team attempted to confront him for a drug test. They had no information about where he was and no other way to contact him. The counselor said that, unfortunately, they couldn't take him back after a blowup like this, and Lisa would need to claim his belongings within the next twenty-four hours before they were donated to Goodwill.

She took a deep breath and put her phone back in her purse. What a night! The only thing she could do was go home and wait for her brother to show up; at least she'd be able to get out of this dress and wash her face. She felt filthy; a creeping dirtiness coated her skin. As she walked down the long, green avenue of trees that lined the Park Blocks, she tried to make herself breathe evenly. This is what she did when she had stage fright: She tricked her body into believing she was safe, that nobody could see her, that she knew what she was doing. She straightened her posture and tried to impersonate a woman who hadn't just been groped by someone she mistrusted and despised.

"Hey," said a deep male voice. A figure sat up on a nearby park bench. "Hey, baby."

Lisa picked up the pace, impersonating a woman who has somewhere else to be. Her shoes slowed her down. She put her hand in her purse, wishing she'd brought mace. Who knew how long it would take for the police to come find her, in whatever ditch this strange man left her.

"I'm talking to you, baby," he said, and his voice was close, making the hair stand up on her arms. He sounded big. Too big for her to fight off.

"Go away," she said, and he burst into giggles.

"Leese, it's me. It's your brother. Calm down, it's just Jeremy."

He came closer, and she saw that yes, it was him, and was so relieved that he wasn't dead or hurt that she burst into tears. He hugged her tight while she squeezed handfuls of his T-shirt, not caring that he smelled like weed or that he'd been hanging out on a goddamn park bench when he should have been safely in rehab.

"You shouldn't get into fights," she said when she'd calmed down.

"You shouldn't wear makeup. When you cry, you get raccoon eyes."

"Those people were trying to help you," she said. "Now what are we supposed to do? Start over, just because you can't follow the rules?"

They walked up Taylor, toward her apartment. The museums and shops were all closed, and their screened windows and grated doors were like blank, watching eyes on Lisa and Jeremy as they passed. Jeremy took Lisa's purse and held her hand. He knew better than to defend himself with her. When they got to her building, he handed over her keys.

"I can find another place for the night," he said, reluctantly. "A hotel or something."

"You don't have any money," she snapped.

"Yeah, I know."

"You should have stayed in treatment," she said as she opened the door for him. He went past her with his head down, looking at the carpet.

"I know."

"They're trying to *help* you."

They went up the stairs and into her studio. She dropped her bag on the floor and kicked her heels under the sofa. She never wanted to see them again.

"Are you mad at me?"

She struggled with her zipper until he came over and carefully undid it for her. The rigid sheath around her relaxed, and she could breathe again. "Of course I am. We had an agreement. We made a plan, and you were going to stick with it this time. You didn't even last ninety days. Why can't you get along? Fighting with your group, fighting with everyone."

"Why shouldn't I fight with them?"

She turned on him, her disbelief making her speechless. Her dress was falling off one shoulder, and she had a run in her stockings. Her mascara was gummy on her lashes and her hair had gone sideways, frizzing into a wad on the top of her head.

"Seriously, Lisa. Why? Just because we have one thing in common doesn't mean we'll have anything else going on. If I learned anything, it's that the person who's most like me is the last person I can trust."

He kissed her forehead.

"I'm glad you're safe," she said. She tried to impersonate a big sister who was ready to clean everything up and be the responsible one, again.

Her brother settled on the couch and picked up a magazine. "I'm always fine, sis. I've got nine lives," he said. "I came back because you need someone looking out for you."

"Do not," she said.

"You're not fooling anyone," he called as she closed the bathroom door.

"You better be there when I'm out of the shower," she shouted back, over the hiss of the running water.

He'd be there; she knew it. That was the thing about brothers. They were no good at pretending. They didn't need to; they just loved you. They turned up like a lucky penny when you least expected them. They saw right through all your little acts.

"I saw Angelina Jolie tonight," she shouted. "She recognized me."

"I guess you're a celebrity now," he said.

She rinsed the suds and styling product out of her hair and let the water fill her ears, temporarily deafening her. She felt normal again, clean, her usual un-done self.

"Don't be ridiculous," she said in her best Angelina voice. "I just play one on TV."

He laughed, doing an impression of someone who isn't worried anymore, and she chimed in, letting the performance catch them both, while the audience who watched from the other side of their imaginary stage melted into applause, and cheers, and laughter.

# THE VOICE OF EDITH

EDITH FROM UPSTAIRS WAS RECORDING a podcast this week. The whole building knew it, because she taped neon-pink notes to everyone's door with the time and date repeated in her loopy-sexy handwriting, asking for quiet. The show had a dumb name that I could never remember. It took an hour, at least. During that arbitrary hour, which always seemed to come at the least convenient time of day, Edith camped out in the laundry room with her headphones on and talked about the Pixies.

Katz and I, who split the shitty, low-ceilinged studio in the basement, could hear every word. This time it was a Sunday night, seven p.m., which was usually my prime time for last-minute laundry. I paced across my half of the apartment while the voice of Edith ululated through the heating duct. She sang and noted to herself where to dub in music or follow up with an interview question. Her laugh was high and artificial. She sounded like one of the waterbirds that crowded the waterfront and shit on the railings of the historic paddleboats.

"Chill," Katz commanded. She passed me a bowl.

This did not change, at all, the speed of time for me. I nudged my laundry pile closer to the door and leaned on the wall. My head was right under the duct—Edith came through loud and clear.

She kept saying the word *trans*; that one was easy to make out. I looked at Katz. "What do you think she's saying?"

Katz shrugged. "It's her podcast. She's saying *trans*."

"But do you think she's saying good things?"

Katz, who was trans, looked up from her Gameboy. "Whatever she says, it's not going to be less than an hour. Cool your jets."

"I wonder who she's talking to."

"*She.*"

*       *       *

KATZ WAS ABOUT TO STOP being Richie when I met her—Richie was the name on the lease for the basement apartment. We connected through a Facebook group for friends living with friends. Housing was almost impossible to find, I'd just started a new job downtown in the Portland Police building, and the Craigslist rental section made me feel as though I was taking a guided tour of my own funeral. Katz offered a private section of the huge basement room for four hundred and fifty dollars, plus half of Internet and utilities, queer-friendly, 420-friendly. The building was a block off Broadway, close to the bus lines. We met in person for the first time at the Peet's Coffee on 15th. Katz got there first.

"I'm transitioning," she said. "I am a she."

"That's great," I said.

"Have you ever lived with a trans person?"

I looked down, ashamed. I had not. I knew that my lack of experience made me deficient, like, as a feminist. "I don't have a problem," I muttered.

"I need a roommate so that I can afford the transition."

"Surgery?"

Katz scoffed. Her disdain made her beautiful to me. Her teeth were gapped in the front, and her lips parted over them in an impeccable punk rock sneer. "That's for rich bitches," she said. "I just want my body to get out of its own way."

She didn't ask me about my pronouns or preferences or make any comment about my perceived level of allyship and queerness. My sister had come out last year; it would have been awkward to chime in and say, *Me too.* So I stayed the way I was. Maybe Katz thought that my appearance spoke for itself. She saw me as an ally, and I didn't try to claim a bigger space than that.

We lived together just fine. Every time I paid rent, I patted myself on the back for helping Katz get a little closer to personal integration.

After that initial meeting, Katz never mentioned her identity, and it was apparent that the role I'd fantasized about—confidante, trans ally, best friend, hand-holder, gender demystifier—wasn't mine to play. Katz wanted to play video games, smoke weed, and leave for work on time. She was so *normal*. I thought I had a highly attuned sensitivity to identity and gender, but Katz threw me off. I couldn't stop thinking about what it meant, trans-ness, and I was primed ideologically to be protective of Katz in every way. But Katz, it seemed, didn't need protecting. Katz was fine. I was the weirdo.

Outside the apartment, though, nobody could tell that I didn't belong. I was a perfect fit for the forensics team, my new boss Jeff said, because I was completely inoffensive.

"I hope that doesn't offend you," he said, as a joke.

I shrugged and tried to smile. I needed the job, and after all he wasn't wrong. I was boring. Average height, average weight, brown eyes, brown hair, average number of freckles, two years of community college, where I got average grades. I was so boring that they didn't bother to drug-test me. So boring that security waved me through the metal detector even when I forgot my ID badge. So boring that one of my former bosses, who'd employed me for eight years, forgot who I was when I called to ask if I could list him as a professional reference.

I could afford rent, and that was about it. I made minimum wage plus ten cents. *Average.*

The only interesting thing I'd ever done was live with Katz. I didn't mention her at all in my interview, although Jeff made a point of saying that Portland Police was an *inclusive* employer, which was code for *Gays welcome, not that anyone would assume you're gay*. So at least he saw me, even if no one else did. The nature of my job made my identity irrelevant. I was a filing clerk, the only one on my team. I spent eight hours a day in a refrigerated room sorting films and entering data into an ancient desktop computer they called Sweeney Todd.

The pictures and numbers were sickening, to say the least. One of the interview questions was, "Have you or a loved one ever been the victim of a sexual assault?" Looking at the photos and lab notes, I understood why they screened out applicants who were survivors. Forty hours a week of this stuff would be immensely triggering. Nothing had ever even *happened* to me, and I had nightmares for the entire six-week training period. After a couple of months, I acclimated, but I still wished somebody would ask me at least once if I was okay.

It was a relief to step away from old Sweeney during my breaks, stretch, and warm my hands on a Styrofoam cup of free coffee. Sometimes there were treats in the break room, and I ate as many as I could and smuggled a few to eat while I hid in a bathroom stall. Food wasn't allowed in the data room. Crumbs attracted ants.

\*     \*     \*

"Have you ever met Edith in person?" I asked Katz.

"I'm on Level Nine."

I fidgeted and went into the tiny kitchen area: a two-burner stove, Katz's butcher block, a utility sink where someone used to clean their paintbrushes, as you could tell by the dry splotches of house colors on the porcelain. I started to heat the water for tea, enough for two. Edith was still going. Being a little stoned was the worst on podcast days, because I felt I was caught in the infinite loop of Edith's voice and that she'd probably just go on talking about every conceivable aspect of alt-rock forever and ever and my laundry would pile up and stink and I wouldn't have anything to wear to work if I left the apartment at all and Katz would move up, Mario World after Mario World, and only I would be frozen in time, waiting for the water to boil, waiting for silence.

I guess I was more of a Talking Heads person, when you got down to it.

I stared into the pot—we didn't have a kettle—and watched the tiny bubbles start to form, like pearls, on the stainless steel.

"You want tea, Katz?" I asked, just to hear someone else's voice, someone other than Edith.

"Level Nine, Dana."

If I served Katz her tea, was I conforming to gender roles? Had Katz ever had male privilege and did she retain any of it as she transitioned? In my heart, I was jealous of her. She had the power to decide her gender expression and, as she changed, she stayed fluid in a way that I didn't. On top of that, she didn't have to explain herself or process anything with me. I was unessential to her transition and, aside from my monthly rent payments, I didn't feel that I fit into the story at all.

"What if she wanted to talk to you? Would you do it?"

Katz put the Gameboy down and took the mug of tea. "Who?"

"Edith."

"Why would I?" She stared at me. Her eyes were an uncanny, milky green. Katz was perpetually single, which was another thing I didn't understand about her. She got prettier every day.

I shrugged. "I'm stoned. I don't know."

"I am the Lorax. I speak for the trees."

She made it sound like a joke, but her stare was hard, glassy.

"I just worry that Edith is putting the wrong ideas out there. You know? About trans stuff."

"No, you're worried that you won't have time to do your laundry."

I was first to look away. Did that mean I was the one who was wrong? I wanted Katz to be on my team, two against Edith, but instead I felt small and alone. We slept in the same room, with our respective beds at opposite corners shielded by paper screens and our bookshelves. Yet I never felt I could win Katz over. I wanted her to see how good I was for her—what an amazing support person, so woke, the best advocate.

"I should just switch days," I said, lamely. "That would take the drama out of it."

"Edith and I used to date. Now we just work together." Katz said. She picked up the Gameboy. "She's fine on the trans thing."

In a world where I wasn't kind of stoned and constrained by my fetishistic relationship to time and space, I could walk right into that laundry room and start my wash, if I wanted to. I had my roll of quarters for the machines. The dryer was the worst, and only warmed my clothes into a soggy, humid bolus. Katz had taken Edith's note off the front of our door and stuck it on the inside. The pink paper kept catching my eye.

"You went out with Edith?"

"Yeah, for about a year. I met her at the call center. We liked each other's voices."

I didn't ask, *Why didn't you tell me.* Why should Katz tell me anything? I felt my face get hot.

"When did you break up?"

"Right before you moved in. She lived here, actually. This is her couch."

We were sitting on Edith's couch. The nubby velvet, bald in places, was the color of a melting orange snow cone. I shifted my weight off its arm. Maybe they'd fucked on this couch. In the four months I'd lived with Katz, making those monthly payments into her transitional hormone fund, it hadn't really occurred to me to think about her sex life.

"Why didn't she take it with her?"

"It didn't fit up the stairs. She's a minimalist, anyway. She's all about giving things up."

I wondered what Katz saw in her, if Katz was still hung up on her ex, if Edith was a regular girl or a trans girl, if Edith was prettier than me. "Do you listen to the podcast?"

Katz snorted. "Same as you. Every week, broadcast live from the laundry room. I know more about the Pixies than is healthy or safe."

I didn't wait, this time. I backed into the laundry room with my arms full of dirty clothes and quarters in my pocket and dumped the whole load on the floor in front of the washing machine without even looking in the direction of Edith's omnipresent, piercing voice. I pulled the washer door open, stuffed in my clothes without sorting them, and slammed it shut. Each quarter I loaded like a bullet into the coin slots.

I kept my soap on the communal shelf over the machines—even though someone used it and the bottle was way lighter than it should have been. The plastic door over the soap trap clattered shut. Edith's voice did not waver; she carried on as though I wasn't even there. *Clunk, ka-chunk.* The water started. Would this be just white noise on her recording? What was the other person saying, the other half of her interview? I put both hands on the cold metal of the washer and leaned against it. I closed my eyes. It was a twenty-five-minute cycle with the extra rinse. With my stomach full of bile, I started to hum a song I didn't know.

"Didn't you get my note?"

I turned and looked down at the source of the voice—at Edith, the person known as Edith, who was sitting cross-legged on the laundry room floor with her huge recording headphones pushed down around her neck. She was the opposite of Katz, full and busty and sweating through her tank top. Her hair was a mass of curls, shaved on one side, the same brilliant, unnatural pink as her Post-Its. Her eyebrows were drawn with purple pencil, and a silver stud dotted her upper lip. She looked like a bitch. She was definitely not boring.

"It's a work night," I said.

"I wasn't finished."

"Okay," I said. "Well."

When I came back to switch my clothes into the dryer, she was gone. No note, even though I expected one, or maybe to find the wet laundry dumped on the floor. But she left no sign, resentful or not. Her microphone and the soft meditation cushion she used were cleared out. The only sounds were someone upstairs flushing a toilet and the counter on the washing machine ticking down from the spin cycle. I shoved my quarters into the coin acceptor. The dryer's white noise ate up the sound around me, pressed against my ears, and turned everything into cotton that turned over and over. Chewing.

*   *   *

Monday morning, I sat in my clean clothes in the coffee shop where I met Katz the first time. I had time to sit for a minute before the bus. Coffee cost one dollar and forty-five cents, which I pinched from my jar of laundry quarters on rainy mornings. Not getting wet on the way to work was getting expensive. Although nobody seemed to notice me, I still had to adhere to a very strict dress code. You couldn't show tattoos, color your hair outside the L'Oreal spectrum, cuff your slacks, wear novelty socks or jeans, or display any piercings aside from one plain stud in each ear. Only women were allowed to wear jewelry, aside from a wedding ring. You couldn't look "unkempt or slovenly," either, the employee handbook said. Spit polish. We worked in a police station, after all.

If you broke one of these rules or showed up more than ten minutes late, you were given a warning. Two warnings and you could be fired on the spot. A clean shirt, without stains, missing buttons, or yellow half-moons under the arms, was essential. I inspected my laundry every week, hoping that I could put off buying new clothes until the next pay period. The number of things I had that were actually work-appropriate dwindled, lost to hot days (sweat), cold days (mud), and rainy days (both). I just had to be careful. If I gave up doing laundry *and* buying my own coffee, it would still take me over a month to save enough money to get a good shirt from a thrift store. I looked in free boxes, but I had a fear of bedbugs. Plus, it seemed wrong to take things that were left out for poor people when I was working and had a place to live.

In the cafe, I was surrounded by couples who hadn't gotten tired of each other yet. Their voices were bird-chatter nonsense that kept catching my ear.

A woman impersonated a mutual friend, "a graduate from the Milwaukee School of Art and Design," while her boyfriend sniggered. A man described throwing a glass of water into a freezing night and how the liquid was solid before it hit the ground. And they were all talking about the housing crisis: five people to a place; new spaces for subletters;

a house that burned and killed someone who was in a hastily constructed money trap under the stairs; the rising rents. But they were all couples who worked. The only other person sitting alone there, a woman in a hand-knit hat, ate what I assumed was lettuce from a takeout box that had "lettuce" written on it in black magic marker. I drank my coffee and thought that all I had was Katz and Katz's goodwill, which did not seem especially reliable.

Drinking coffee the consistency of apple juice, I looked around for the clock, accidentally making eye contact with the lettuce-eating woman. It was 7:30 in the morning.

*This* was not where I'd wanted to be when I set out. I made it to the bus on time but as I was getting out my ID to show my pass, I fumbled my coffee cup. Its plastic lid popped off. I felt the liquid soak through my clean shirt.

I didn't have time to get off the bus, go back, and change. If I even had a clean one. I had to choose: punctuality or dress code? I couldn't have both. My shirt was soaked in coffee. My last white shirt.

I RODE ONE STOP AND pulled the request cord. I walked the extra six blocks back to the apartment with my arms crossed over my chest as though I was cold, even though this was spring, warm enough for a skirt without tights.

I inserted my key and felt that the door was already unlocked—the pins didn't click back when I turned the key, and the latch, when I pushed on the metal plate, wasn't all the way fastened either. I'd never come home in the middle of Katz's work day. Maybe she'd left it open during a trip upstairs to check the mail or for some small domestic chore I didn't get to deduce because, as I leaned into the room with my free hand already fumbling with my shirt buttons, I saw the patch of fur between Katz's legs: a dark sunflower partially obscured by the fingers of Edith, white as worms, which led to Edith's pale arm and her naked breasts, to the barbell in her nipple which glinted like the stud in her lip, which, as she perceived me, peeled back in a sneer or a smile, I couldn't tell which, and maybe I wasn't meant to know, because Katz lifted her head from its gorgeous repose against the cushions of the sofa that I'd always suspected was a site of Edith's pleasure, looked me dead in the eye, and said, "Dana, what the fuck?"

She did not close her legs. I froze, trying to fixate on the exposed pipes on the ceiling. "I need to change," I said. I couldn't make myself say I was sorry. I scuttled to my corner of the studio—its open floor plan suddenly *too* horribly open—and hid behind the bookcase I used as a privacy screen. I stripped off my stained shirt and dropped it and then stood there shivering, staring at the folded pile of clothes in the milk crate I used as a dresser. I couldn't force myself to choose one; I couldn't think about colors, or even time, which slithered past me, making me later and later for my shift at work. My ears were trained on the entwined forms of Katz and Edith, listening for the subtle movements of their bodies, their murmurs and whispers, the sofa's creak as they slowly uncoupled. Then, a sigh, and the door closing. The shirt I selected was blue, with Western-style flowers embroidered on the collar. It was not work-appropriate, but it was the only one I had left. I went back into the living room. My heart trembled.

Katz, zipped up in her usual place, sat with her feet on the coffee table and the Gameboy on her lap. Her long fingers tapped the buttons.

"I'm sorry," I said.

"Level Ten, Dana."

"We don't have to talk about it."

She looked up at me as I hesitated by the door. I was late, really late now, and I felt it in the sweat that was starting to pool under my arms. I should have called in to let them know, but now I was truly behind schedule and I could lose my job for this, I could lose my place to live, and worst of all I could lose Katz, who was so beautiful to me that my eyes stung when I looked at her, whose mouth was moving and saying words I didn't understand, as though she was another species entirely, a creature more graceful and poignant than I would ever be and not at all human. I felt small and sweaty and jealous.

"The rent's going up this month," she said. "We got a letter."

"I think it's worth it," I said.

She shrugged. The situation wasn't that simple now, and we both knew it. The Gameboy chirped, and she switched it off without saving the level. She'd have to start over from the beginning now.

"You're easier to live with when you're not here," she said. "That was part of our deal, right? That you would have your life and I would have mine. Separate."

"You want me to be invisible."

My voice cracked, but she nodded and kept nodding. My throat closed.

"I don't really want to talk about it anymore," she said.

I had no words.

"You can go now. Please don't come home until after six. You're paying for my space, right? Not my time. This is just until I can finish transitioning."

I had fifty-five dollars in my bank account. I had maybe no job. I lived on tea and discount canned food, eggs, fun-sized candy bars from the reception desk at work. This was temporary only because I couldn't sustain it. I licked my lips.

"I can do that," I said.

Katz smiled at me, for probably the second time ever. "It means a lot," she said. "Your support. I don't know what I would do without you."

BY THE TIME I GOT to work, I had my excuse all figured out, but it didn't matter, because the apartment building on the corner caught on fire. Someone had left a candle burning. After they left for work in the morning, the candle set their bedroom on fire. The whole apartment burned and spit huge, rainbow-tinted flames out of the breaking windows. Everyone got out safely, but the whole block was evacuated.

My coworkers were standing across the street in a huddle, gossiping, watching Emergency Services hose down the smoking wreck.

"Dana! I'm so glad you're here," Jeff said, taking my arm. "Where were you?"

"In the back. I forgot to clock in," I lied.

"That's fine, I can check you off my safety list. I was so worried. I thought you were still inside." He turned to the rest of the group. "Dana's here," he announced.

Nobody noticed I was wearing the wrong kind of shirt.

"It's so good to see you," said one of the other techs. "You ready to work late today?"

"Every day," I said. "If I lived here, I'd be home by now."

That made them laugh, and I knew I was safe. I stepped into their circle and stood there like everyone else with my hands in my pockets, listening to their jokes and half-remembered headlines and opinions: This fire was just a sign of more trouble for the housing market; no, it meant people needed updated buildings to live in, not these gorgeous old husks; no, it was just an accident, plain and simple, there's no such thing as an act of God, that's the first thing you learn in this business. They turned, contemplated the burnt building's blackened architecture and smoldering roof. The problem was deeper than this, they agreed; this was a sign of something, some deeper flaw in the city's infrastructure, housing allowance, cost of living, population density. Although what did we expect, moving to Portland, in the flood zone of a major tributary? The city was all timber when people came here. *Stumptown.* This fire stuff, this is the Wild West. We just had to be careful, watch out for each other. There weren't many places to go. We'd lost how many units, up in smoke in a matter of hours. Anyone's home, anyone's safe haven could be next. Look, the ashes are falling. It's like static, black snow, and it's landing on people.

If I kept quiet and let their words filter past me, it wasn't that different from the radio, or Edith's half of her weekly podcast interview, a voice in another room, speaking a language I couldn't seem to learn or understand no matter how hard or how hopefully I pressed my ear to the vent's metal grille. On the other side was everything I wished I knew. I heard and waited for the meaning to follow.

# HOW TO BE A BETTER METAMOUR

THE MAGAZINE SAID, IF YOU want to know him better, get to know his other lovers. As Josie, age twenty-six, read the block of text, her brow crumpled. *Third Wheel* was her favorite advice column. Her boyfriend, Mark, had suggested it to her after he came out and she was having trouble accepting him. *I just want you to know me better*, he'd said and texted her the link to *Third Wheel*.

Mark was polyamorous. Where Josie grew up, in Ohio, that was called cheating, but Portland and everything about it was different from Findlay. She felt awkward and vanilla here. The people were different. The rules she was used to didn't apply. Dating, which she did with the help of a few apps, felt like a series of interviews in which she was either hiring and nobody was qualified or she was answering questions that made her feel profoundly old-fashioned. Everyone was poly here, except for Josie. At least, that's what Mark told her. She believed him.

His other lovers, *Third Wheel* said. The column called these outside people "metamours." The lover of your lover. Even dating was a way to network, to polyamorous people. You slept with someone, and they slept with someone, and you built a community on your willingness to fuck each other. A metamour was also called a co-husband or co-wife or a familiar. Josie wondered what it would be like to be married to someone who had another wife. She decided she would probably kill both of them.

"What are you reading? Your cheeks are pink," Mark said.

"I got hot all of a sudden."

He smiled. He was thirty-three. He looked older to her—laugh lines around his eyes—and even though she knew that theoretically they were both young, and that when she was thirty-three she'd see her present self as a child and other thirty-three-year-olds as normal people, she wondered what he really knew that she didn't, aside from how to love more than one person at a time.

"You're pretty when you blush."

She smiled, but he went back to his crossword puzzle. "I wasn't blushing," she muttered. Nothing in *Third Wheel* talked about how to tell if you were too grown up, or not grown up enough.

AFTER BREAKFAST, MARK WANTED TO go back to his place and fuck, but Josie made up a story about how she needed to help her roommate with a really important project. She had a hard time saying no to Mark's bed, but it was summer and she didn't want to get all sweaty; besides, once they started fucking, it was so hard for her to stop she'd spend all day in his bed in the loft of the carriage house, with the skylight open to let the fresh air in and her happy sounds out. Mark kissed her for a long time after she unlocked her bike from his house's front fence.

"I wish you'd stay."

"What will you do instead?"

"I'll get up to something," he told her. "Liz and I have plans tonight."

"Plans?"

"There's room for one more, if you want to join us. We're taking a picnic to Overlook Park to watch the sunset."

"That sounds romantic." She tried to keep the sarcastic tone out of her voice but knew from Mark's expression that she'd failed.

"We're dating. I wish you'd just accept her. She's important to me too."

"I hope you have fun." She swung her leg over the bike's crossbar.

He sighed and rubbed the back of his neck. He wasn't from Portland, either, but he wasn't from a place like Findlay. "Look, Jo. I'll text you her number. If you were willing to meet—maybe it would put some of this to bed."

Put it to bed. She knew he fucked Liz in the same bed as her, on the same sheets. In this warm weather, she sometimes smelled the other woman's oils and her shampoo and soap on the pillows. Liz smelled like geraniums and roses and lemons softening with mold. When Josie thought this special combination of scents was Mark's, she couldn't get enough of it. Now, it turned her stomach. She wished he would at least do the laundry between Liz's visits. She wished it was winter. She wished that Liz wasn't even in the picture.

Her phone buzzed against her hip as she pedaled away. That would be the phone number. Mark did all the things *Third Wheel* said to do: He told her about Liz, including her last name and where they'd met, and he told Josie when he had a date with her and where they went. He seemed too eager to share the details and frequency of the sex he had with Liz, which made Josie feel even sicker, so sick that she actually almost fainted when he said that Liz gave amazing head and, even though Mark didn't get the point, he could at least shut up about how *open-minded* Liz was so that he could bring Josie a glass of water. She was, he said, a little green around the gills.

*   *   *

JOSIE'S FUTURE SELF, WHO WAS thirty-three and way more open-minded than Liz and Mark put together, would probably look back on this period of her life and sigh wistfully. Wistfully, or whimsically? She always mixed those words up. Mark didn't ask for her help with the crossword because of that. She turned down Albina and then took a left. The bike lane went all the way into Sellwood, the other end of Portland's universe, where she rented a room on the first floor of a house near the college. The long ride took at least thirty minutes, which gave her time to think about nothing as North Portland's industrial, glass-fronted shops and gentrified store facades gave way to green spaces. She rode along the Springwater Corridor, inhaling the sweet scent of grass and growing weeds and the vague, brackish scent of the Willamette River just down the low bank.

Some of the trees here were the same and some of the birds, but on days like this Josie felt her new city's foreignness, as though she was on another planet entirely, hearing sounds and smelling smells that were reminiscent of the place she grew up but on closer examination were only similar enough to Findlay to compel her senses and lull her into a feeling of familiarity. No matter which way she looked, she couldn't quite convince herself that she was home.

*   *   *

SHE LIVED WITH ASHLEY, TWENTY-SIX, Caitlin, twenty-five, and Jenna, twenty-nine. Jenna seemed at times impossibly old and mysterious and spent most of her time off in her room reading about crystals and testing various plant emulsions. She was an aesthetician who spent her days ripping hair out of women's bodies with hot wax and tweezers. Her boyfriend was a bartender who rode a motorcycle. Ashley and Caitlin, who worked at the same nonprofit, were uncoupled but sometimes brought strange men back to the house and had loud, enthusiastic sex with them. Josie, at home, felt her white-bread-ness. Even at home, she felt out of place.

She parked her bike on the house's front porch and went in as though entering a temple. It smelled like basil and popcorn—cooking. She dodged into her room before anyone could see her and closed the door. She sat on her bed, took out her phone and set it, screen up, on the bed. She folded her legs and stared down into its flickering face as though consulting an oracle.

Liz Bechtolt. And a phone number. She typed the name into Facebook and thumbed down the scroll of faces, wondering which one was Mark's other girlfriend. He explained one time that polyamory wasn't infidelity, because what he did with Liz didn't change how he felt or what he did with Josie. And he said that it couldn't be a betrayal, because he'd been honest with both of them the whole time—he hadn't gotten bored, changed the rules in the middle of the game, decided to switch ponies. Josie's stomach clenched. He had not gotten bored with her, true, but having another girlfriend in the picture, or even saving a space for someone else, seemed to mean that he had no intention of really letting her in, either. He had room on his plate for a dab of each partner, mayonnaise and mustard, and that was enough for him. He said all the time that Josie was free to see other people, but she didn't want that. She was afraid to move any farther from Mark, to give up more of him than she already had. She was as close as he would let her be, and it wasn't enough.

Of course all the Facebook Lizzes were very pretty. She hated that she was this kind of girl, who got jealous. She hated that she was the kind of girl who did the things she did and felt how she felt. She wished to be older, wiser, grander, but seemed unable to change or be anything other than what she was: too young, too self-aware, too naïve. She felt as though she was surrounded by girls, but still without friends. Nobody loved her brand of vulnerability here.

Her first text was designed to be innocuous, a wrong number kind of text that could be read and deleted without comment.

*Hi, how's it going?*

She sent it and then put the phone down. She could tell Mark she'd gotten in touch the way he wanted. Then maybe he'd stop bringing it up. In the kitchen on the other side of her bedroom wall, one of her housemates turned the water on. She heard Caitlin singing, indistinct. Outside was a lawn mower, someone doing yard work before the heat of the day came on too hard.

The text window flickered. Liz had read receipts. Josie watched the speech bubble, three percolating dots, appear on the left side. Then: *Hi, Josie! I'm getting ready for work, then my date with Mark.*

Next line: *Nice to hear from you.*

It had a weird finality to it. Liz already knew her name—that meant Mark gave her Josie's number first. Why hadn't *she* been the one to reach out? Josie turned her phone's screen to the quilt and lay back, arms crossed. She felt that she was playing a game whose rules she didn't know. Was Liz his favorite? The primary? How exactly did you talk to your metamour when you didn't want to?

As the sun set, Josie knew, Mark and Liz were sitting down next to each other on a picnic blanket at Overlook Park. She imagined Liz in a pretty sundress, the kind she saw in the window at Urban Outfitters or Anthropologie, totally out of her price range. They'd have a picnic basket with separate compartments inside, a chilled bottle of champagne, and no mosquitoes.

Josie lay on her bed, watching the sun move in pinkening stripes down the wall. The stars would come out, and they would hold hands, counting them, making wishes. The love Mark had with someone else was always a little better than whatever he had with Josie. The lighting was better, the makeup, and even the script—as though her little slice of relationship was merely a dress rehearsal for what he was doing with her metamour. She wondered, not for the first time, what he said to Liz, and if they were the same words he used with Josie. Did he hold the other girl's face the same way? Did he put his lips against her ear when he fucked her, whispering, urging her to cum? By the time she'd thought it all through, she was too sad to masturbate and fell asleep with her clothes on.

When she woke up, it was maybe four in the morning. Her phone vibrated next to her ear.

*Come over.*

It was Mark. She picked up the phone, stared at it. She didn't have read receipts.

He must be alone, then. Or he wanted a threesome. Fuck him. She turned the phone off and rolled over. When she woke up again, the birds were singing, and Jenna was running the coffee grinder.

"Wow, you're up early."

"I can't sleep. It's too hot."

Jenna nodded sagely. Her bedroom was pretty much the whole basement, the coolest room in the house in the summer. The unfinished ceiling was hung with dreamcatchers, hides, horns, and dried flowers—a witch's bower.

"My boyfriend is dating someone else," Josie blurted.

Jenna frowned.

"I mean, obviously I know about it. But I've never done this on purpose before. You know?"

"So he's poly."

"Everyone is here."

Jenna poured two mugs and passed Josie the carton of cream. "I'm not. You don't have to do anything you don't want to. Is he really that great?"

The coffee tasted slightly of cardamom and was the perfect temperature. The kitchen window was open, to let in the few hours of cooler, fresh air. The pale-yellow curtains, which belonged to Jenna and were embroidered with small golden stars, waved in the barely-there breeze. Josie sighed.

"He's your first real one, huh," Jenna said. "Have you met this other bitch?"

"I don't even know her." She didn't know why Jenna, whose whole witch thing was built on a neo-feminist ideal of radical sisterhood—the label *witch* itself, Jenna once explained, stood for Women's International Terrorist Conspiracy from Hell—would call Liz a bitch. The word floated in the air, green as swamp gas, and its presence made Josie feel just a tiny bit better. Even Jenna saw it. Liz was a bitch. They didn't have to know her to decide they didn't like her.

"Meet her. You'll see that whatever you're up against isn't much." Jenna topped off her mug, which was painted with red-capped mushrooms. "God. Men are the worst. The one you're dating has got to be a moron."

"Why?"

Yes, Jenna, please tell me why he is a moron, because I can't quite put my finger on it.

"He must be. Otherwise, how could he think you'd stick around for this game? You're young, you're new, but you're smart too. This is the thing about men," she said. "Once you stop giving them what they want, they change what they ask for. No man has a hard limit. But we do, women do. We're the ones who set the boundaries in relationships. That's our power."

"Shouldn't men and women do that equally? Like, an egalitarian relationship?"

Jenna raised a perfect eyebrow. "There's no such thing as an equal relationship, because men and women are not equal in love and never will be. Balance is key. Not equality. If it's really bugging you, though, you could do something about it. There's a vacant lot on the corner with a bunch of groundsel growing in it."

"Groundsel?"

"Tall weed, looks like yellow daisies. Dig up one of the plants with a tool that has no iron in it and touch your heart five times with the plant. Spit three times after each touch, and the cure will be complete. Technically, it's for toothache, but you know, whatever works."

She went downstairs, and Josie heard her put on a record, then close the door that separated her bedroom from the rest of the basement. Josie finished her coffee, rinsed the cup, and left it clean and upside down on the rack. She felt strange and empty. Jenna's words rattled around in her brain. Her chest ached as if something rotten was collapsing inside her.

She picked up her phone and typed Liz's name into the message screen.

*Wanna get coffee today?*

She saw the read receipt appear, then the response, which followed almost at once. *Sure! I'm leaving Mark's right now, headed to Sweetpea Bakery.*

Jeez, that's cutting it close, Josie thought. But she was almost dressed, and the idea of meeting Liz at this moment, with her mind so quiet, was tempting.

*I'll be there in 20.*

She put on her favorite T-shirt, the black one with the screen print of Marilyn Monroe's face, and made sure her socks matched. She picked out a necklace, a crescent moon on a long silver chain, and when she slipped it over her head she felt some of Jenna's witchy power transfer into her. She walked her bike to the corner and saw the groundsel growing knee-high, thick as wheat in the vacant lot. She had no tool, aside from her cell phone, so she picked a handful of yellow flowers and crushed them against her heart. They released a bitter scent that nauseated her. Her tongue swelled. She spat three times, between her feet, letting her saliva dribble out of her mouth as though she was drunk.

She threw the ruined flowers back over the chain-link fence into a place where the grass and weeds were flattened and dry.

As she rode, she repeated the mantra Jenna had provided. *Bitch.* Even though Josie wasn't the superstitious type, she felt her perspective align with Jenna's. What was Josie even doing? Was this imbalanced triangle ever going to straighten up and magically deliver her the thing she wished for? She tried to imagine Jenna in her situation and found it impossible.

If it wasn't enough, it wasn't enough. She didn't have room in her life for more disappointment. Weeds grew; people picked the best ones and killed the rest.

Sweetpea was a small vegan bakery tucked into the trendy strip on SE 12th and Stark next to a vegan minimart, a vegan tattoo parlor, and a vegan-owned acupuncture and massage clinic. Josie locked her bike up at the rack out front, amazed that the steel tubing was already warm from the sun. She didn't know exactly what Liz looked like or what she would say to her, but she was glad she'd come. She felt a little less afraid, just being there. *I'm leaving Mark's right now,* Liz had texted. So she spent the night in his bed; so they slept late. But for once Josie did not feel jealous of either of them.

*Is he really that great?* Jenna had said.

"Josie," someone said when she walked into the bakery, blinking the glare out of her eyes.

The woman was standing by the counter, with a white paper cup in one hand and a small plate in the other. "I'm Liz. I would hug you, but my hands are full."

Josie looked down into Liz's face. She was smaller, softer, older than Josie expected. She looked like a kindergarten teacher. "It's fine. How about you pick a table for us?"

"I didn't think you'd get here so fast," Liz said as Josie slid into the chair opposite her. She couldn't stomach sweets before noon, so she had a bagel, smeared with some kind of imitation vegan cream cheese that actually wasn't too bad.

"I'm in Sellwood. It's not far."

"I love that neighborhood." Liz sank her teeth into a peanut butter bar that immediately covered her plate in brown sugar crumbles—a kindergarten teacher eating a graham cracker. Josie noticed that her arms were covered in indecently thick dark hair. A glance at Liz's face, which was appealing and plain, showed matching patches on her temples and even on her upper lip. Her black bob had a fading blue streak in it. Her brows were unplucked. A week ago, she would have been intimidated by this woman—her metamour—but now she viewed Liz through Jenna-colored glasses and all she saw was a not-very-attractive woman who made no effort to make herself even a little bit beautiful. Liz was not her competition. Josie looked closely and saw someone who was willing to compromise on what she wanted because she didn't have enough power, or enough confidence, to barter for it. Liz was sticking around for the game, had stuck around, and Mark was comfortable keeping her waiting for whatever it was she wanted.

"How was your picnic?"

"So pretty. Mark says that the two of you ride through that part of North Portland a lot."

"We don't," Josie said without thinking. She picked a yellow petal off her arm. "I don't know why he would tell you that."

Liz put her cookie down. "He was eager for me to meet you."

"I don't know why he would be eager." Josie laughed, half at how ridiculously good it felt to tell the truth and half at the look on Liz's face. Josie's bluntness was out of place in Portland, just like her need to love only one man, only one at a time, and not share him with anyone ever.

Liz smiled. She was better looking when she smiled, even with her hairy arms.

Josie said, "We can't just sit here and talk about Mark."

"No," Liz agreed.

"I mean, he's not that great," Josie said. "And he would like it too much."

That made Liz laugh, and then she was pretty, but Josie didn't mind, because her chest stopped hurting and she knew that Jenna's spell had worked and, as of this moment, she didn't give a fuck about Mark and honestly Liz could fucking have him, since it was clear that on some level Mark and his half-baked theory of polyamory was the best she could do, and if that was what Liz wanted to settle for, then who was Josie to stand in her way? She imagined Liz waking up next to Mark under the carriage house's skylight and hugging him while he checked his dating-app messages and texts from Josie and tried to confirm a happy hour date with some other bitch for later that day. And this picture wasn't pure imagination because he'd done exactly all of those things in the presence of Josie, even while she pressed the length of her sleep-softened body against him, waiting impatiently for him to put the phone down and turn to her and give her the attention she desired. If Liz wanted all of that, all that non-affection Mark had to offer, it was hers.

"I see why he likes you," Liz said.

"I see why he likes *you*," Josie said. "I'm glad he gave you my number."

"Me too."

"I mean, I hope we stay in touch, is what I'm saying."

Liz's eyes widened. "What are you talking about?"

"I'm breaking up with him," Josie said. "Like, effective today. He wasn't giving me what I needed. But I would love to have coffee or something again."

"Are you serious?"

"I should probably let him know, huh?" Josie said.

Liz blushed, picked up her cookie, put it back down, picked it up. "This isn't how I expected this to go."

"I don't even like the word *metamour*," Josie said. "I don't like this arrangement. But that's not on you. It's just not enough."

"Do you want me to tell him? You're going to tell him."

Josie shrugged. *Third Wheel* didn't give instructions for how to leave a poly situation. In the column, these relationships seemed to live on indefinitely under the constant attention and nudging of the people in them. But she didn't *want* to be friends with Mark or slowly transition from being his girlfriend while he fucked other people and she shopped for a suitable replacement. She didn't want to talk about labels and names. She wanted a love that was simple and worthy.

"I'll let him know. Just pretend it's a surprise, okay?"

Liz smiled. "You seem a little surprised yourself."

"I had a change of heart, is all. Plus, meeting you. I think it's the best choice for everyone."

"Why would meeting me change that?" Another small sprinkling of brown sugar fell onto the plate. But her eyes were not composed, and, with a delicacy that did not come naturally to her but was undoubtedly the gift of Jenna's powers, Josie saw Liz's excitement, her eagerness. Josie was granting Liz's wish. The only thing Josie had to do was make sure that Liz was in a position to enjoy it.

"You're so much better for him than I am," she said. "I have no idea how to do this kind of relationship. He's happy when he's with you, and I think that once I'm out of the picture you'll get to see more of each other. He needs someone like you for the long-term."

And Liz's smile was glittering now, and she was beautiful, really, wearing her hope all over her face. "I feel the same way," she said.

And then they changed the subject and talked about movies.

MARK CALLED A LOT OVER the next few days and texted, too, but Jenna gave her a crystal to put on top of her phone to filter out negativity and, after about a week, Josie stopped hearing from him. She felt relief, honestly. She rode her bike in the sun until she got freckles on her shoulders and her nose and she ate sandwiches in the park and went to bed alone and whenever she felt like it.

At night, before sleep, she lay in the dark with the sheets kicked off, her hands traveling over her warm belly. Outside, she heard a car start, and then the hazards and red brake lights flashed in gentle pulses through the blinds. She was not lonely, here in the dark with herself. She was alone, a network of one, a single dot connected to nobody.

When she touched herself, she saw not Mark's face but a swirling void full of fingers and tongues that thrust into one another, licking and pulling, and this vision was what made her cum so hard that her bed shook, knocking her phone to the floor and sending the borrowed rose quartz skittering under the bed. She picked it up, her hands still sticky with lube, and the screen blinked on.

*Best week of my life*, Liz said. *I hope you're enjoying it too.*

Josie typed a yellow daisy and a golden heart. *Yes*, she wrote. *Actually, I think I'm in love again.*

# CAT SITTING

I KNEW I LIKED KIM when she said hi at the AA meeting, complimented my crop top, and told me I reminded her of Debbie Harry. Her exact words were, "Debbie Harry, if Debbie was played by Michelle Pfeiffer, by the way I'm Kim and I have cancer." Who wouldn't want to be friends after that?

Kim was straight, but I didn't hold that against her. Something about coping with her own mortality gave her dimension, kindness, intuition. They're the qualities I associate with people of my type, not hers. Most straight people are so clueless. They ask such stupid questions. *What's it like being gay?* They watch porn actors fucking each other in same-sex couplings and they think it's an anatomical thing, the way I feel and am. Nubs and fists and getting married and making babies. That's their *normal*. It's exhausting. *What's it like?*

You tell me.

Kim said chemo was exhausting. She missed her long hair and hated explaining to people that she looked okay because she had a rare neck cancer, not the usual kinds, but, in reality, I don't think she had anything to complain about.

Who wouldn't want her life? I did—cancer or no cancer. I told myself that hers was the life I should be living. It was like one long Instagram story. Kim was a designer. She drove a black BMW. She traveled too much for work, and I was part-time at the Audubon Society, so we figured something out. When she was gone, I was supposed to collect the mail, feed the cat, and make it look as if someone was home. It was convenient for her, and, since I was sober, she figured she could trust me. It was an easy job, and her cat was the best cat. Biggie was a massive white furball with crossed blue eyes: a sweet little bitch, even if all cats *are* heartless, murdering bird killers.

Not that I have a resentment. They can't help the way they are.

*   *   *

My girlfriend dumped me the morning that Kim left for Brazil.

I don't really want to dwell on the breakup, but I was eager to get away.

I treated Kim's house as though it was mine. I wasn't stealing. Well, yes I was, but she always left a note that said, "Help yourself," and I chose to interpret that in a way that suited me. Why shouldn't I enjoy it, while I could? I deserved it, anyway. My feelings were hurt.

Kim's blender was rad, in part because she couldn't eat or swallow, but also because she could afford the best one. I made myself an organic blueberry and almond milk smoothie that tasted as if it came from a field of wild, native fruit bushes. The blender did something to bring out the honey in it, and the sunshine. Rich people really do have it better. So do their cats. Biggie pooped in a special odor-proof box in the laundry room. She ate better than I did.

All of Kim's stuff was high tech. Even her supplements were spray vitamins. Pumpkin oil and cherry-flavored B12 and Omega-6 blend and St. John's Wort and belladonna and THC and CBD and two kinds of prescription anti-anxiety drugs and some kind of liquid cocaine were all lined up like perfume samples.

I totally didn't mean to relapse, but I did two squirts from every bottle. Then I lay down on the bed. When I woke up and went back into the bathroom to hit the vitamins again, I saw that I had eyeliner all over my cheek, the same inky black as Kim's phenomenally fancy sheets. I lay on the bed spraying vitamins into my mouth and alternately crying about my breakup and fantasizing about getting revenge on my ex. Biggie sat next to my head. She wasn't allowed in the bedroom because of Kim's immune system, but I always ignored that and just left the air filter running and the windows open. I wasn't worried about cat dander at all. The filter was super-efficient. Stains, on the other hand, were a different story.

\*     \*     \*

I WAS MAKING ANOTHER SMOOTHIE when Biggie went out through the cat door and came back with a meadowlark in her mouth. It was still alive, which I didn't realize until Biggie let go of it. She brought me a present.

I looked at her, and she meowed.

"What are you thinking?" I asked her, and that's how I knew I was super fucking high, because who wonders what a cat has on its mind. I realized I still had the bottle of B12 in my hand. My pee was going to be really, *really* orange. Biggie's pupils were huge, and mine probably were too. She was high on the bird's suffering. She wasn't going to kill it yet. She saved its death for me.

The meadowlark fluttered around, as though beating itself against the fireplace or Kim's hi-fi would somehow change its situation. Biggie pounced on it again and let it go, chasing it over the linen sofas and across the buffalo-hide rug. She clawed loose pawfuls of quills, feathers with vanes, contour and flight feathers, down, filoplume, semiplume, and bristle. They pooled in the corners of the living room and under the shelves and cases. The meadowlark flapped into the wall and then through the door to the place where I'd been sleeping.

I followed. A songbird couldn't hurt me. At work, I helped reset the broken wing of a great horned owl, and its beak was like garden shears. It could have punctured the meat of my hands without even trying. Humans are so soft, just buttery animals with thin hides and flat little teeth, no claws. We have no natural defenses. We're just fucking *mean* to each other.

When you're high, don't call anyone, especially not your friend who has cancer. I sat on the edge of the bed and stared at the bird. It was nearly wingless now. Biggie lay down at my feet and we watched the bird make Rorschach blotches on the wall.

Hell yes, I was going to leave it there.

"Aren't we just fifty kinds of awful," I murmured.

She purred.

# FIELD MEDICINE

RENT WAS DUE, SO I did my makeup and took my card table to the farmer's market. My hand-lettered sign said *Spirit Healing, Love Signs, Femme Magick*. Each tarot reading was an easy twenty bucks, and all most people wanted was to feel as if someone was listening—and the sparkle, the magic. For readings, I wore my candy-pink wig and painted glitter triangles on my cheeks and forehead. I looked like something from a world where human kinds of trouble don't exist. My femme power was real too. Its vibe was big and rosy and sympathetic, and people were drawn to it like butterflies to blossoms.

That's what healed people: kindness. When I held someone's hand, they immediately relaxed. What I did was field medicine: not a permanent solution, but the help that gets you to the thing that will save you. The in-between help that, no matter how small, can turn the tide of a person's life.

I set up my table and did a quick meditation, trying to dispel the jitters that had kept me up worrying. The day before, Gloria's mother had fallen down the stairs and shattered her skull—an actual tragedy. Gloria never let me read for her. Even if I'd seen her mother's accident coming, I don't think I could have told her. Between getting her into a cab at midnight and worrying about my rent, I was energetically drained.

After I centered myself, I brightened my smile and beckoned a few women toward my fortune telling booth. I made money easily because of my Capricorn rising sign, but my Mercury was too close to Pisces.

Easy come, easy go. My friend Jenna told me that my problem was, when I had money, I never knew what to spend it on.

When their readings were done and I'd tucked the money into my shoe, I reached for my phone to see if Gloria had called. Nothing. I put the phone back in my purse and when I looked up, Sophie, holding a canvas bag stuffed with kale, was standing over my table. In spite of all my banishing rituals, she was here in my booth: Gloria's ex.

She sat down and folded her hands on my table. "Hi," she said.

"I don't do palm readings," I said. "Cards only, and it's twenty bucks. Cash."

She nodded, slid a grubby bill to me. I put it under my lucky obsidian owl and started my opening spiritual patter while I sized up old Sophie.

That morning, she looked tired. She wore a wristwatch and a braided sailor's bracelet whose shabby strings had felted into one dull hank. She was too young for her clothes, which belonged on a middle-aged woman: gray, deep blue, bamboo, cotton, wholesome. Her cis-ness was cloying, offensive.

She had curly, terrier-colored hair and a puppy-dog nose. I couldn't imagine her in the leather collar Gloria used to put on her, or the rubber pony gag. The fuzzy socks in our toolbox of toys must have been Sophie's size, since they didn't fit me. Those and a vibrator still sticky with lube and her body's oils, a nylon bondage rope. What I knew about her private life was at odds with the fresh-faced girl who sat across from me.

Although she didn't know it, Sophie had been a fixture in my life since I started dating her ex. Gloria told me, right off the bat, that she wasn't completely through being in love with Sophie. I said, *I don't care; I don't really date butch girls*, just to let her know I wasn't getting invested. I said, *How can you be rejected by someone who never wanted you in the first place.*

No matter how tight my boundaries were, information leaked through them: Sophie's birthday; her favorite restaurant; little things that I tried to ignore, even though they made my tongue itch. When Gloria told me Sophie's name, I laughed. "That's her name?" I said. "That's a dog's name."

Because I thought I was safe. I was wrong.

I drew red stars on the sidewalk outside Gloria's house, praying for relief from *her* obsession. It worked, but the energy that lingered around her flowed into me, filling me, until I was the one who couldn't stop thinking about Sophie even when I wasn't awake. I knew that Sophie was not gone, but a ghost, clinging to the edges of my life. For the first few months of our relationship, every time I fucked Gloria, I felt as if I'd been inside Sophie too. Sometimes I woke up in the middle of the night, certain I could hear her breathing.

*   *   *

"Do you have a question in mind?" I asked, after I'd explained the three-card reading and said a quick incantation to invoke the insight of Athena.

She nodded.

"You don't have to tell me, but it's helpful," I said. A flake of glitter fell on the velvet cloth I used to decorate my table.

"Someone I care about is in a lot of pain, and I want to know if I can do anything about it," she said. "A lot of pain. The worst, maybe. It's just so sad."

"What is?"

"Impermanence." She looked at the food cart next to us, decorated with a rack of pastel-painted vintage ice cream scoops; the menu was scrawled under them in chalk. "This will all go, someday."

I nodded. I didn't mind. One day, she would be dead. I would be dead. The people we loved, separately or together, would be dead. This park would be condos populated by people who had never heard of any of us. "They tell you, when you decide to love people, to buy a black dress," I said. "Because you'll wear it to a lot of funerals."

She rubbed her forehead.

"Think about death, and I'll cut the cards," I told her. I divided the tarot deck into three equal parts. She watched my hands, as if expecting me to do a parlor trick with them.

"I lost three friends in the last six months," I offered, though she hadn't asked. "It's an occupational hazard, being trans. High risk. We get sick, or somebody murders us. The grief doesn't get easier, but it does make me value the days that I have with each person I love."

"I don't know any dead people," she said.

*Of course you don't*, I thought. *You're a child.* We weren't just different; we weren't even the same species. For me, life was tempered with joy. Pain was inevitable; suffering was optional. My grief did not limit me or make me averse to feeling more love. By the time I was Sophie's age, I'd gotten used to it. I'd lived in my car before I'd miraculously found an apartment. I had to lie about my gender on my housing application and also to get food stamps. I'd considered going back to sex work to make ends meet. I couldn't legally travel, get married, receive medical care, apply for a passport, donate blood, choose the bathroom I wanted to use, or adopt children. I'd lost more friends than I could count to overdoses, suicides, and "accidents." I was dating a butch, cis woman for the first time in a decade. I paid my rent by trying to read someone else's future in a deck of cards. I was forty-three, past the life expectancy for my demographic: old, for a trans person. And yet, my life was beautiful. I wanted to tell Sophie that. I wanted to say, *Pain doesn't always mean you're in danger; sometimes it just means you have a decision to make.* I could easily have ended up like her, had I not, at one time, chosen to be brave.

I shuffled each of the three stacks of cards while she talked. Her voice was low, like mine, and pleasant, soothing.

Once, before cell phones, Sophie told me, her mother had stopped at the grocery store on her way home from a day trip to L.A. It had been a short delay, but in the hour past the expected arrival time, Sophie had worked herself into a panic. She was in the grip of adolescence and still living at home. She used the phone; she called the people her mother had been to see in L.A. She called emergency rooms and transportation services. She convinced herself that her mother, an older mother than other people's mothers, had gotten into a horrific accident on the drive back to Ojai and was, in that hour, creeping in and out of consciousness, crushed into the tin can of the family's Saab.

*You got yourself that wound up*, I said, but Sophie did not hear me because she was still talking. She tugged at her curls. I'd found strands of her hair by Gloria's bed. If I'd been a different kind of witch, I would have collected them, put them in a mirror box, and filled Sophie's life with smoke. I turned over the card on the top of the first stack. The Tower.

She was an orphan whose parents weren't dead yet.

"The Tower, reversed, is the sign of false fear. We assume that our pain is a symptom of something deeper. A splinter that feels like a spear." I put the card in front of her on the table. I tapped the flames that erupted from the peaked roof of the citadel and the bodies flung from it. "See? *Reversed*. It can stand for resisting change, anger that festers."

She looked down at the picture on the Tower card as though it was an image of a real catastrophe. I reached for the second stack of cards, feeling certain I could read her mind or had enough information to make a highly educated guess.

*       *       *

NO MATTER WHERE I WENT, Sophie cast a blue shadow on me. Last summer, Gloria hiked with me to the first summit of Dog Mountain. Sitting beside her, I cut juicy slices from a mango and looked down over a field of wildflowers. Beyond that was the Columbia River, a luscious blue that caught the shade of the summer sky and threw it back onto the evergreens lining its banks. It was a perfect day. The mango juice attracted bees to my hands. Later, Gloria would let me diagram her star chart, then ignore everything that I intuited for her, saying she didn't believe in fancy hoodoo. Typical Libra. The breeze from the valley blew up the mountain, cooling our sweat. She wanted to talk about her ex, and, since apparently I had no way to avoid Sophie, not even on a mountaintop, I listened.

As our relationship grew, time eclipsed the loss of Sophie. Gloria talked about her less and less. Maybe the red chalk stars were working.

I burned purple candles and meditated, visualizing a huge, pink eraser removing Sophie's outline from my life. Her presence became easier to tolerate. The hole where she'd been healed. When Gloria reached for me at night, I knew it was *me* she wanted. She held me and told me that one of the things she admired most was my strength.

"You never feel sorry for yourself," she said to me. "*You're* not a victim."

Of course I heard the comparison in her voice.

So I was strong for Gloria, even when my heart was hurting. I was the calm one when Gloria got in a cab in the middle of the night without kissing me goodbye. I texted her my love and compassion when she said she would have to take her mother off life support. Leaving. Always hard. *My* mother stopped speaking to me the day I came out. We didn't exist for each other anymore. Sophie would say she understood Gloria's pain, because one day, *her* mother would go away too. Maybe she was right. I was the one with no mother to bury.

"It's natural for children to outgrow their parents. It's a law of nature," I said, drawing the King of Cups. "Are your mother and father happy?"

"Happy? I don't know. They don't tell me things. They don't want to worry me."

I laid the King of Cups next to the Tower. "A positive sign follows a painful one. This king is gentle, and this card promises a balance of masculine and feminine energy. Together, the two suggest that it is time to heal imbalances or to find a calm anchor in a storm of anxiety."

"So you're saying that my friend will come through this? That it's a good thing?"

"It's all a matter of perspective."

"I don't see how death could be anything except sad," she said.

"Was the dead person someone you know?"

"We were supposed to meet," she said. "It just never happened. And now I guess it never will."

Her voice shook on the last word. I saw self-pity move over her face like a silver ripple and under it, anxiety. She knew just enough about life to know that she should be afraid. The cards had that power over people too; they could reduce people to tears or coax them into divulging secrets, dreams they'd never told anyone. Jenna, who taught me to read tarot and many other things, told me that our real power is helping people remember who they were before they decided to be grown-up. This was the opposite. I perceived Sophie's deeply held womanhood. Her maturity was dying to come to the surface, but she kept it submerged, bubbles dribbling from its mouth.

She was a mermaid, half of two things that wanted to kill one another, always divided.

*     *     *

"I DON'T KNOW WHAT I'D do if she said she wanted me back," Gloria said one time.

I licked my lips. My head was still fuzzy from sex. I couldn't believe what I was hearing. "What's to know?"

I rolled over. She followed, putting her arm around me, drawing me close.

"You're my favorite," she whispered in my ear, Sophie's ear, every girl's ear.

*     *     *

"MY MOTHER HAS A DEATH plan," I told Sophie. "We've been talking about it since I was in high school. If I don't follow it, she says she's going to haunt me."

"Really?"

"That's not in the cards, though," I said, trying to lighten her mood. I liked to bring the third card out with an affirmation; it helped people feel as if they got their money's worth. "And this reading isn't about me, it's about you."

"Are you sure about that?"

I felt the vibe shift, and the hair stood up on my arms, all the way to the shoulder. Suddenly, it occurred to me that the energy lines that connected me with Sophie might be two-way. My phone jingled, but I didn't pick it up. I knew what that call was.

A moment later, Sophie's rang too.

"I'm not answering," she said. "We both know what she's going to tell us."

I turned over the third card, the Eight of Swords. A blindfolded woman, wrapped in chains, stood in a ring of swords, symbolizing self-imposed immobility. My fingers itched, so I turned over the next card, too, crossing the Eight. The Lovers: a relationship, gained or sacrificed.

The reading started to click into place; shapes darted through my brain.

"You are my mirror," I told Sophie. "And I am your reflection. When we refuse to see ourselves clearly, other people reflect to us the aspects of ourselves that need nurturing. That's the good, bad, and ugly. Not just the self we wish others to see."

There is a difference between transparency and vulnerability, I thought. Vulnerability is not a performance. It's a transfer of energy or understanding, an experience that transforms the listener's understanding of the speaker. It does not require total honesty. What it does need is truth, which is something distinct from the terms we use to define ourselves. Vulnerability occurs in the temporary absence of fear, the natural reluctance to *be seen*. Vulnerability does not announce itself: It does not say *Look, I'm So Brave*. It expects nothing in return. True vulnerability, I realized, is a pure act of love that momentarily punctures the illusion that we are unconnected, inviolable, alone.

"You're not afraid of losing people," she said.

"I am. I don't grieve for people I've never met. I can't take the whole world on my heart, right? Is it anyone's responsibility to carry that?"

"Gloria asked me to come to the funeral, when this is all over."

I spread my hands over the cards' faces, covering them. I felt a low buzz in my palms that vibrated through the table and down into the earth. I could sense the trees around us, tall elms and maples digging their lumpy, twisted roots past the concrete and through the living, breathing foundation that connected us to one another. Sophie's nervous energy touched me, but it was only a small, passing twitch. I ignored it, going deeper.

"Will you go?" I asked. I didn't need to tell her that I wasn't invited.

"I can't," she said. "It's too hard. I never was that person she could lean on. I think the worst thing is showing up for somebody and then completely falling apart."

"You feel guilty."

"Of course I do. Everything about her makes me feel guilty. I can't go, though, and I can't figure out how to tell her I can't."

*Why does she want you there and not me?* I thought. I looked down at my hands and the pale webs between my fingers. I didn't belong on this planet. This kind of place could not be my home.

She cleared her throat, drawing me out of my trance. "I didn't come here to bother you. I do appreciate the insights. I wish—I just wish I had what you have. Your strength. You're not afraid of anything. I wish you could tell me your secret."

"It's simple: I don't put my pain on a pedestal," I said. "I don't worship my pain. If I gave it more attention than the absolute bare minimum, I'd go insane."

"No matter who it is? Even the people you love most?"

"Even them. When it hurts, that means it's real. If I feel guilt, it means I am not truly caring for someone. I'm bound to them by fear. Love is natural, so it's free of all anxiety."

She frowned at me, and her eyes were blank.

An inventory—like an invoice or a tax return—is transparent. It is only facts. It lies because it refuses to admit that there is a deeper story. I had plenty of facts about Sophie, but they didn't add up because she didn't know who she really was. She didn't know how to be vulnerable, so I couldn't help her open up. She bit her lip, and I realized that she was probably very good at talking to her therapist.

"They could die at any moment," she said.

"But they're not dying," I said. I tapped the cards with my nail, pointing out the path to safety promised in each one.

It would have been cruel to say, *Some people have real problems.* Maybe I should have told Sophie the truth: that her problems were imaginary, that they were the natural consequences of the way she'd set up her life.

But I didn't say those things. The situation was simple. She was in pain, and her pain defined her, and she was entitled to her pain, and the world was entitled to help her bear it. What really hurt her was her inability to make decisions for fear of the pain that might follow.

There wasn't a card for that.

"Not today, I guess," she said. The reading was over; I felt it. She reached for her bag of kale and lifted it onto her lap. She looked at me over the bouquet of massive, crude green leaves. "I'm glad I got to meet you."

"Are you going to call Gloria back?" I asked. Our girlfriend's name hovered between us. Its syllables twisted in the air. I scooped the cards into a messy pile and squared their edges, getting them ready for the next person who needed their help. "Let her know about the funeral?"

"She didn't ask you, did she," Sophie said.

"No."

"If she did, would you go?"

I considered. "No."

"Why not? She's your partner now. The thing we have—I don't think it's built to handle that. It was supposed to be for one summer, not three years, you know?"

"She still called *you*," I said.

"I just don't think I did anything to deserve it."

*Me neither*, I thought. But acting with mercy was part of my business. I looked at her again, noticing how her face was softened by a few extra pounds. She looked settled. The armload of greens couldn't be just for her. She was taking care of someone else: not Gloria.

"She should have told you what was going on," Sophie said. "I'm sorry. I can't apologize for her, but I can say it for me."

"She tried," I said.

"She does that." She left my table. I watched her disappear into the crush of people that always packed the market. In a moment, I couldn't tell her apart from any of the others. She was a stranger again, in dull earth tones, taking organic vegetables home in her bike panniers to cook with care from scratch because one small, thoughtful act might avert an apocalypse, if you did it with kindness; it's true, you could prevent the worst. That's where my money came from: reminding people of their power, the best thing inside themselves. In every tragedy might be a grain of love and in every love, disaster.

# PAS DE DEUX

"AND THEN HE SAID, YOU know you're the prettiest girl I've ever seen."

"Really?"

"Yeah, really. And we were standing like this." She moved close to me, really close. I could feel her breath. "Here, you be me, and I'll be him." She put my back against the wall, just to one side of the framed Degas print we'd gotten at a thrift store.

"And then he started, like, this." She touched my shoulder, slowly pushing it against the wall with her body.

*This is Amanda, who is just my roommate,* I thought. She pushed against my other shoulder. "And then he did this," she said. She didn't check my face for a reaction.

Over my shoulder, next to my ear, the Degas ballerina held her foot in a perfectly balanced arabesque. The foot was pointed at my head, and I felt it like a loaded gun.

This is Amanda, and I only got to say her name once before she stepped into me, rose up onto her tiptoes, and bit my face, soft then hard so I could feel her incisors making impressions in the soft tissue over my cheekbone.

"He did this to me." She held me behind the neck.

"What else did he do?" I asked, but my voice was getting sticky and her face was so close that I couldn't see if she was smiling or not.

"Let me show you," she said. We slid down the wall in a grand plié and she showed me, slowly, what he did to her.

# SHINE OF THE EVER

## MATING

The year before the year I quit drinking was one of the last, best years of my life.

The drinking wasn't great, obviously. But everything else was. It was 2006 but it felt like 1998, just before everyone discovered my hometown and Portland became a "destination." That year is special to me because it was the last time the city and I were really *together*, in the way that couples and families and best friends are together.

Every moment from that year is like a pin on the map in my heart. It's a red thumbtack on the corner of 19th and Jefferson, for example, marking a place where I once had a sandwich with someone who left for Istanbul the next day.

Like Portland, he was someone I loved and will probably never see again.

The patio where we drank syrupy root beers and teased each other about being young and dumb is gone now. It's condos. Future condos, anyway. The sign out front says each unit starts at a very affordable half-million—*each*.

The sandwich was a Reuben, for the record. We split the pickle.

Since I got sober, Portland has done nothing but break my heart. I stay. It's where everything that ever mattered happened to me. The last year of my drinking, I was twenty-three, but still not ready to grow up.

Neither was Portland. The city and I were flexing, testing our limits. We were both at the end of what felt like very long and sheltered childhoods.

In retrospect, everything I said and felt and did at twenty-three was not unique, except in that it happened to me. Who *wasn't* a mess in 2006? I believed I'd never get any older, back then. I didn't believe that Portland or I would ever change. Every time another vacant lot filled up with high-rise apartments or another historic building was razed and replaced by a parking garage, I felt as if the world was ending.

I mean, it was. It kind of still is.

*   *   *

IN 2006, I ONLY EVER met girls in bars. I'd just gotten dumped by my first real girlfriend: a straight girl, go figure, but those were easy to find. The Egyptian Room was the only lesbian bar left in Portland, and I didn't go there. I was too young to know what I was missing. The E-Room closed in 2010 and was replaced by another, less awesome bar called Weird Bar. That's when Division Street was still someplace where you could stumble along for blocks without seeing someone my age. There were a couple minimarts and a reptile and insect pet store which we hypothesized was probably a front for the mafia. (Which mafia was never clear, because we were too chicken to go inside and snoop around.) The E-Room is a fucking collage gallery now. It's called Collage. They have monthly "clip-ins." They sell framed pieces for hundreds of dollars—scraps of leather and expensive paper—and magazines about collaging. *Curated art and craft supplies*. Unbelievable. I have no idea how the fuck they're still in business and the entire lesbian population of Portland couldn't keep a fucking bar open.

Anyway, Division wasn't where I did my hunting. When I was ready to get over Alison, I went to North Portland to find girls of my type.

I was still smoking then. Unfiltered Luckies. I locked my bike up in front of the Crow Bar. A girl worked there sometimes, and she was pretty, and she'd smiled at me once or twice. I ground out my cigarette under my shoe, exhaled the last breath of smoke, and stepped inside. I'd had my eye on this girl for weeks now, and it was time to make things happen.

In the empty bar, I'd have the red-felted pool table to myself. I had nothing to hide behind, no noise or people. I considered backing out. As much as I liked day drinking, it was easier to sneak in during busy hours, when she would be distracted, when she might not notice me watching, checking to see if she was straight or not. I heard a clink of glasses below the bar.

*Yes.*

I put a few quarters in the jukebox and got the triangle. That was one of the things I did in those days: I played a lot of pool and I always had a roll of quarters in my messenger bag. Most of the pool tables in town were garbage, because drunks leaned on them or stupidly burned them with cigarettes. They were uneven, out of true. You could only get good on a table if you got to know its quirks: the invisible hills and valleys in its felt, the way the center pocket couldn't hold a ball with English on it, and the way the rails were quick or slow to move the cue to its return. I spent a lot of time playing with bent cues in dive bars all over town. I wasn't great, but I knew which way each table's bed was made.

The Crow Bar had a nice setup: free to play during off-peak hours. I could pace myself, make her come to me. I set the rack, cracked it. I lined up my first shot, pretending I wasn't the only customer, and knocked around a game of nine-ball.

"Mind if I play winner?" she asked.

She had materialized at my elbow and offered me a pint of beer. Surprised me. I took it and handed her the pool cue. She bent across the table: three ball in the corner pocket. I looked her over. She was exactly what I wanted. I gulped half the beer and wiped my mouth with the back of my hand. I felt loose, good-looking. There's a reason they call it liquid courage.

"You're going to whoop me, aren't you," I said.

"Absolutely," she said. "I'm a real shark."

Her name was Ada. She looked so much like Alison—the narrow nose, dark lashes, freckles—that I let myself forget she was a stranger. She was both familiar and fresh. I just needed to get the taste of Alison out of my mouth, clear my system. Ada would do.

That should have been it: a one-night stand with yet another pretty bartender I wouldn't call and didn't mind never seeing again. I had a notebook of phone numbers that I "lost" or "found" depending on how lonely I felt. Something about Ada stuck with me, though. I liked her. She was sweet.

Our first time was amazing, and the second one was even better. That's how hooking up is, and also why it never works: Sex is always better when the other girl's in love with you.

## BED

On Ada's birthday, her phone started ringing at like eight in the morning. We didn't get out of bed to silence it until the fifth or sixth call. Around noon, it rang again, and she picked it up, held the power button until the screen went gray, and dropped it into the pile of her clothes by the foot of the bed. I rolled over; my head was on her pillow. I was trying to write a poem, but it was turning out to be more of a letter. I was bad at poems, anyway.

"Who's that?" I asked.

"My friend. Arthur."

"How come you didn't answer it?"

She sighed and pulled the covers up to her shoulders. A magazine, spread open at a Gucci ad, rested on her knees. The model's pubic hair was waxed into the house's logo. "He just wants to have coffee or take me out for birthday brunch."

"You should go." I sat up on one elbow. "We spend all our time at my place. You should hang out with your friends. Don't you want to celebrate with them?"

She flipped the page of her magazine. Her phone beeped: a voicemail. She ignored it and kissed me on the shoulder. It was as if she was deaf to anything that wasn't me. She started doing this every time we got together.

Her birthday was her personal new year, and Ada had made it clear she wasn't interested in changing anything.

"You gonna call him back?"

"If I feel like it."

I lay back, laced my fingers behind my neck. The bare dogwood branch outside my window shivered with starlings. "I just don't want you to feel like I'm keeping you here. Plus, I didn't know it was your birthday until yesterday. I didn't get you anything."

She flipped again. A whiff of perfume sample. "I want to be here. I want to be kept."

I smiled at her, caught her eye. "I'm your present," I said.

"We belong together," she replied, smiling back. "I don't want any distractions."

The starlings lifted off together, a flapping, screeching net.

I asked, "What was your last partner like? Before me?"

She put her hands flat on the magazine, started to tear out one of the pages. "That was before I lived in Portland. His name was Greg, and we dated when I was going to Oberlin. We were in studio art class together."

"You dated a guy?"

"Well, he wasn't perfect," she said. "He was from a nice family. Canadian. He spoke fluent French."

I pictured Ada carefully sketching a reclining nude. I'd only ever seen people do that in the movies, always as foreplay. I tried to imagine Greg's face. I tried not to feel weird about her attraction to men. Her identity was a red flag and it made me super nervous. Alison left me for her best friend, Stanley. She never even kissed a guy before Stanley. The whole two years we dated, she'd sworn that she was completely gay and not even curious about switching teams. She told me I was stupid to be jealous. Well, I was stupid, because I let her shame me into believing her. Look where that got me.

I was not interested in going through *that*, ever again.

"How long did you date Greg?" I asked.

"Just until I dropped out. It wasn't a good time for me. I wasn't a talented enough artist. *Very* depressing."

"So, you moved to Portland, where it rains almost every day."

She laughed. "I like the rain. And besides, now there's you."

I kissed her arm as she started to rip a second piece of paper. The glossy paper quivered, rippling as she tugged.

"Your turn," she said. "Full disclosure."

"Oh, it's pretty boring. There's not much to tell. Actually, that's not completely true. The last girl I dated decided that she didn't love me anymore. Left me for a friend of hers."

"Names?"

"Whose?"

"Theirs," Ada said. She aligned the pages, straightening the corners.

"Her name was Alison and his was Stanley. I guess they're happy together, as happy as you can be, dating a guy." I tried to laugh, but my throat was suddenly dry. The poem in my lap looked as if it was written in tally marks instead of language: just garbage.

Ada closed her magazine and settled against my chest. "Not happier than we are, though." It was a statement, not a question.

"No, not happier than us." Her curls tickled my neck. She pulled the quilt over our heads; the gray, warm dark covered us like a tent.

## I LOVE YOU

We spent most of the winter in and around my apartment, which overlooked a boring section of southeast Belmont, before the cafes and PNW-inspired restaurants moved in. My rent back then was five hundred and fifty dollars a month. It had hardwood floors, a bedroom, pocket doors, *and* a view of Mount Tabor. My neighbors were older people who had been there since the 1980s. I was the youngest person in the building, young enough that I was the only one who didn't have a player for the tapes the other tenants swapped in the laundry room "library." I only had a binder of CDs. I didn't buy a lot of music, because at the time the rent I paid was considered kind of high. Since then, it has more than tripled. I'm pretty sure my old neighbors are all out in the Numbers now. I'm just saying. I don't live there anymore. Nobody I know does, but there's never a vacancy. Explain how that works. Where the hell do all these new people come from?

At least the weather hasn't changed. That winter with Ada, it mostly rained, but one day snow piled like popcorn in the gutters, and on another morning a white fog muffled the neighborhood so that we couldn't even see the mattress company storefront across the street.

We were a *we*, an actual couple. We did relationship things. Ada went to her classes at Portland State, and I went to my library job, but we always met up at the end of the day. She didn't want to spend time with anyone else, and I wasn't bored yet, so it worked. She served me free beers when she picked up shifts at the Crow Bar. When school got too busy, she quit, and started bringing over a bottle of whiskey a couple times a month.

She didn't want me to ever feel deprived or like I was missing out, she said. She didn't want me to have a reason to go anywhere but home.

We went to places that are other places now. We shared beers at Blue Monk, which was a bar and music venue where you could hear actual good hip-hop and jazz musicians who didn't play that gooey, elevator shit. The Blue Monk is called something else now, and there's a line out front with a doorman and a velvet rope. The people waiting are all dressed up. Lines were never a thing, back then. I associate never waiting with that time of my life, because the timing was always just magically perfect. Anything you wanted, you could have right then: brunch, beer, a turn in the horseshoe pit. Delayed gratification didn't exist, when I was twenty-three.

Ada and I kissed in bars that are too clean for me now and too expensive. It's bizarre, when I go back now and try to approximate the proportions of the places I used to know so well. I went to one of my old dives a few years after it closed, and only the ceiling was the same. Pipes and drywall, peeling paint, that was all. Everything else, from the lighting to the tinted mirrors over each booth, was *styled*. The weird thing was, the place was styled to look like Old Portland. My Portland. They spent a fortune trying to do it too. The matching frosted globes that hung from the exposed rafters would run at least four hundred apiece. A matched set in such good condition must have cost a mint. The tables were tropical salvage. I had that feeling I was in a movie set of my own living room, where every object looked exactly like my personal possession but nicer, cleaner, and more appealing. I hate it. These designers put in a lot of effort to make things seem natural, but I think the only people who believe it are the ones who never saw the original. They don't understand that this isn't Portland anymore: it's *Portlandia*. A theme park of the places we used to love.

If you have no point of reference, you are very easy to fool.

Ada had her own corner in my apartment now, but not her own key. We never went to her place. She transferred clean clothes into the bottom dresser drawer. Her sketchpads cluttered the foot of the bed. Her toothbrush leaned against mine in the glass. I let her get closer, telling myself that it meant something, that I could approximate the thing I'd already had and lost.

"Tell me about Alison," she asked over coffee before work.

Stumptown was busy that morning; the stools around us crowded too close. The brassy-haired woman next to me stepped on my coat, tugging it off my chair to the slushy linoleum. I wasn't prepared to have this conversation.

"I'd rather not."

"It's a simple question."

"It's private. Another time."

She seemed to be more comfortable in loud places, though she herself was quiet. She'd first said *I Love You* at a Sleater-Kinney show, while we were squeezed together against the front edge of the stage. I didn't believe it until she repeated it later into my ringing ears. She seemed to seek invisibility but then asked me awkward questions in public, cornering me. As though, if other people were listening, I was more likely to be honest.

"Was she pretty?"

I sighed. "In a cheerleader kind of way, I guess."

"Blonde?"

"Not as pretty as you." I stuck my finger into the foam of my latte, disturbing the heart-shaped leaf. "I'd really rather not."

She pouted. In profile, she resembled a young Liz Taylor, her freckles the color of mud.

I said, "We can talk about something else."

"Why? What's so sacred about it? You said I could ask you anything."

It wasn't the right time was all, what with the brassy-haired woman clicking open her cell phone, a blind man with his Labrador letting in a burst of snowy air, and the steam wand on the espresso machine blotting out the voices around us. I knew Ada didn't perceive these things as disturbances; they were a diversion, a smoke screen. I let the foam prickle on my finger. I told her enough to convince her I had no secrets. She wanted to believe me and so she did. The stories, of course, were paper thin. I wasn't actually giving her anything. I'd built a veneer over myself, changed the lightbulbs. I was still the same old Jamie. I just looked nicer from the street.

## NEW YEAR'S EVE

I broke the pattern the night Ada stayed late at school, finishing a final paper for Chinese Literature. It was New Year's Eve and, although she'd said she could come dancing with me, although she'd already agreed to be my lucky midnight kiss, she needed to be in the library instead. She was apologetic on the phone, but I could tell she preferred her homework. She didn't like parties, it turned out, and hated bars, anything that meant leaving my apartment and spending time with other people. I was sick of it.

I tried getting drunk at home, but it didn't work. The bottle she'd left at my place was barely enough for a shot on the rocks. I finished it off while I paced back and forth, getting more and more antsy. I hadn't realized how fucking bored I was. I tripped over a pair of Ada's shoes and kicked them out of the way; one flew into a corner, and the other under the bed. *Fuck this.*

I went down to the lobby and called my best friend Ted, who never made plans until the last minute. We had met a while back at Satyricon, which opened the year I was born. That night, Ted was wearing his pineapple-print collared shirt, tucked in, with a belt, and Top-Siders. I think his shorts had pleats in the front too. At a punk show. He looked like a complete asshole, which he kind of was, and I knew we were meant for each other. We'd been friends ever since. I don't remember what band was playing that night; we saw a lot of acts there. Satyricon ended up closing in 2010. I was sober but I still mourn its passing. The bar was one of the last institutions from my old days to go: the longest running punk venue on the West Coast.

Ted was still an asshole, though.

"Ted," I said.

"Jamie. When are you going to get your own phone?"

"*Ted.* I'm bored. I'm out of booze. Let's go someplace."

"Any old place?" he teased.

"The older the better. No hipsters. And likely to still be in business next year."

We agreed to get together at Huber's, which opened in 1879 and was still selling turkey legs, flaming mugs of Spanish Coffee, and mashed potatoes. The tables were crowded with the usual New Year's partiers, middle-aged people wearing crowns, calling out the time as we got closer to midnight. Noise filled the place like a balloon, bouncing off the stained-glass ceiling and the cartoonishly large clock by the bar. In the back room, a piano player pounded the meaty chords of "Lady Madonna."

"This place is the number one user of Kahlua in the U.S.," Ted said, laying the bar menu flat. He eyed the bartender, a skinny girl with long bangs. She wore a man's black vest; her shirtsleeves puffed out like angel wings. Huber's was one of the only places where staff had to wear a uniform. For once, I didn't mind. Too much was changing, these days; I craved any kind of tradition.

I said, "That's disgusting. I hate Kahlua."

"Too bad, because that's what we're having. Your resolution should be to try more new things." Ted signaled and ordered two Spanish Coffees. With a flourish, the girl poured long plumes of rum, coffee, and cream into mugs and lit them with a match. The couple next to us applauded. I took my drink and rolled my eyes. Why were people so corny?

"I hate new things."

"Quit sneering and let people have their fun. It's the signature Huber's drink," Ted said.

"How do you know that?"

"Google." He slid his credit card across the counter. "Keep that open, will you? Thanks."

A few drinks later, I didn't care as much that I was surrounded by straight people and crammed against the corner of the bar. The piano player switched to "Oh! You Pretty Things" and I sang along when he hit the chorus. I didn't have a great voice, but it didn't matter because Huber's was packed to capacity and so loud that even Ted, whose ear was right by my mouth so we could half-scream at each other, could barely make out what I was saying.

People jostled behind me, and I caught a whiff of vanilla.

Ted pulled my sleeve. "Oh, hi, Alison."

I tipped my head back.

"Hi," I mumbled. "Happy New Year."

"What're you guys doing here?" she shouted over the roar of the bar. She was smiling. "I can't believe they let you in."

"Ted's paying," I said, enjoying the fact that I could still make Alison laugh. She'd changed her hair, but something else was different. I couldn't decide exactly what. We hadn't spoken in more than a year. And yet, she still made me dizzy. I saw all the instant signs of trouble, like the way I couldn't make my eyes go anywhere except to her.

"I'm here with Stanley," she said, waving to a man at one of the crowded booths. He lifted his hand hesitantly. I wanted to punch him in the mouth. "I can stay for just a second."

"You look good," Ted said. "Doesn't she, Jay?"

"Always," I said. The beads of her necklace swung close to my cheek. Her shoes were high golden heels with a cluster of imitation sapphires over the toes.

Ted gestured for another round of shots. "You sure you and Stanley won't join us?"

She shook her head. "No, I've gotta go," she said. "But the three of us should get together. Like old times."

"Maybe next year," I blurted, and it took her a moment to catch the joke. The shot glass in front of me wavered. *Gotta make way for the Homo Superior.*

"Next year, for sure. My number's still the same," she said, as if we both knew there was no way I could forget it. She bent, quickly, kissed my cheek. "Happy New Year, honey. I hope it's a good one for you."

"She didn't kiss *me*," Ted said.

Down the street, at the Tube, Ted kissed four girls and I kissed none. It was a straight bar, and anyway I was too drunk to do more than keep drinking. Alison's lipstick smeared on my sleeve as I rubbed my cheek, trying to clear my conscience. I called Ada from a pay phone at midnight, but everyone was singing "Auld Lang Syne" so loudly that she couldn't make out who I was. She hung up on me.

Ted gave me money for a cab, but I just pocketed it and decided to walk home. I went the wrong way for a few blocks before I realized I was going in circles. Downtown, three in the morning. The new year put a snap in the air, and across town I could hear the fireworks popping. I sat on the marble steps by the library's massive doors and stretched out my legs. The sky was almost clear that night. The clouds parted to show jagged streaks of stars.

I tilted my head back, trying to make out a familiar constellation. The library was a white fortress engraved with the names of the great thinkers, but inside, they'd converted everything to data, all computers and machines. I suddenly missed *my* card catalog, the one we had at work. Inconvenient as it was, it had character. It made you slow down, think about what you really wanted. And if you knew how to ask the right questions, it could give you the answers.

My head drooped, and I snapped it back up. I couldn't sleep here with the bums. I wasn't too drunk to make it home—not tonight. I could manage it, I thought, if I was careful.

I'd been with Ada for five months. I'd waited for her to love me as Alison did, make me feel the way Alison did, step into the Alison-shaped hole in my life. It wasn't working because it wasn't the same. Time kept rushing by me, and everything I loved slipped away just as I sank my claws into it.

I walked home long past two a.m., stumbling over the uneven sidewalks. I stubbed my toe on a tree root and yelled *fuck* at the sudden pain. There were no streetlights in these neighborhoods. Everything was gray. The leaves were long gone, and thin clouds now obscured the stars. I stopped at my building's doorstep and stared. Was this where I lived? The strange light dulled it, making it look unfamiliar. I was relieved that my key still worked, that my bed was empty and cool.

**ADA**

Spring midterms, rain. Ada came home soaked. She wrapped her textbooks in plastic, but the rain still dampened them. She spread the dimpled pages in front of the heating vent. Though she still hadn't invited Jamie to her apartment, it felt strange being there without her.

She turned on her radio, the volume low, and boiled water for tea. It had taken her over five years to do three years of work on this art history degree. She'd transferred twice. The student loans piled up. She was taking Chinese classes this year and, although she had no trouble with the characters, she'd learned that she was tone-deaf. Every exam was an exercise in humiliation. She practiced alone with her hand cupped over her ear so she could hear her own clumsy pronunciation. Her friend Arthur offered to tutor her, but it didn't work. They always ended up talking about other things in English. He had a new job at a real estate company, photographing properties as they went up for sale, one by one. It was a good job for an artist. Houses were a hot commodity, even the tiny bungalows full of dry rot and bad insulation. He was suddenly making close to six figures, shooting homes and cars that he could almost afford to own himself. He invited Ada to work with him, take a cut of his fee, be his assistant, maybe dinner after, you should see some of these properties, they're palaces, aren't you curious?

He liked her. She let him.

Outside, it rained bullets. Ada knelt by the vent and started to study with a finger on each sound. Her phone waited by her elbow in case Jamie called. Jamie had been hard to pin down. She always had an excuse for why she was busy. She needed more hours this month, so she was working late, or Ted needed something, so they were going out for a drink. She and Ada spent fewer nights together than they used to, only once a week at best. Ada hadn't had a chance to replace the last bottle of whiskey she left at Jamie's. *I'll invite her over here soon*, she thought, and she could make them both breakfast the next morning.

While she was puzzling through a workbook exercise, her cell phone rang. She was relieved to have a break.

"Hello?"

"Hi," Jamie said. The caller ID: *Pay Phone*. "I'm out at the bar."

"With Ted?"

"Yeah, with Ted." Ada heard a woman's voice in the background and laughter. An indecipherable rock and roll song pumped raggedly from a jukebox. "I'm heading back to my place late, but I'll see you tomorrow, okay?"

"Well," she hesitated. "I thought you could maybe come over here. Stay over."

"Tonight? I don't know. I'll be out *really* late. I don't want to wake you up."

"But you've never been here before." She cleared her throat.

"Well, maybe another time? I want things to be good between us, you know?"

"I never see you anymore."

"Another night, I'll come over. You saw me yesterday." The woman's voice again, her laughter. Was she with Jamie? Was she signaling to the woman, spiraling her finger around her ear, rolling her eyes, trying to get away from the phone?

"Who are you with?"

She sighed. "Ted. Remember? I invited you too."

"I'm busy." Ada bit her lips until she felt the fibers inside them crunch between her teeth. "You know I've got a test."

"Then you'll probably see me again tomorrow. It's not a big deal, Ada."

"It matters to *me*. Why can't you come now?"

Jamie sighed. "Listen, I have to go. I'll call you tomorrow morning."

But Ada didn't hear from her for three days. Even though she biked to Jamie's apartment, rang the buzzer, waited in the rain. Her heart ached. Her tongue thickened through her Chinese midterm. The professor shook his head.

"Is something wrong?" he asked in Mandarin.

"No," Ada replied. "My life is very full."

He switched to English. "If you wish, you may retake the exam next week. I would like you to do well in this class. I know you are trying."

She thanked him and squeezed her book to her chest. Her eyes stung. At home, she stared at her cell phone. Her flashcards were neglected on the end of the bed. Jamie didn't call and didn't call. Ada slept through the night with the phone, silent, under her pillow.

## LOOKING

When I woke up, I told Ada I wasn't feeling well. It wasn't difficult to convince her. I was usually sick in the morning, back then. I couldn't shake my chronic, low-level hangover or cover the circles under my eyes.

I pretended to be asleep as Ada got ready for class. When she left, she kissed my forehead. I waited half an hour to make sure she didn't come back for a forgotten book. It felt nice to lie to her. I never really felt like myself unless I was being a little bit dishonest. I'd been avoiding Ada long enough to get used to having my privacy again. If she complained,

I doubled down with more nights out, letting Ted buy me lap dances and pay for my whiskey. Every time Ada asked me for *more*, I cut another trapdoor in the life I was building with her.

I lay back against the headboard, daydreaming. The comforter cocooned me. I was so drowsy. When we were still sleeping together, Alison used to press her nose against my ear. She talked in her sleep, and her words echoed in my skull. She murmured through my dreams. I hummed, shutting my eyes. I imagined her in our bed with one of her hands under my pillow and the other between my legs. I let myself remember the old days—when we thought it would last forever. As I touched myself, I pretended my fingers were hers, as though I could invoke her this way, and my sense of her made her feel real, even in this bed, where the pillows still smelled like Ada's hair. When I came, it rattled through me like a train in a nightmare, gathering speed, bringing the past sickeningly close.

After, my skin was warm, and I fell asleep again, though I didn't mean to. When I opened my eyes an hour later, I felt groggy and sad. I didn't like waking up alone. In the shower, I felt guilty for the amount of time it took to rinse the shampoo out of my hair. What Ada didn't know wouldn't hurt her, or me. The trick was, I didn't give her a reason to suspect anything. She was so naïve; she believed everything I told her. She thought I was whoever I was pretending to be.

I picked out my lilac Breeders shirt. Alison always said it was her favorite. I combed my hair back and put on my sunglasses. Then I was out the door; my heart felt strangely tight.

Sweet-talking Alison into meeting me for coffee wasn't easy, but I'd done it. Since New Year's, I'd called a few times, just to talk. Time had passed, I said. I missed seeing her and I wanted to catch up. Just to check in. No hard feelings. It's been forever. She bought my act and agreed to come to the east side on a weekday.

Only straight women think you can go back to being friends.

We met at the Stumptown on Belmont. It's still there, but a decade later when Oregon legalized weed, the mural of purple dogs chasing a yellow, sun-shaped ball got painted over with an ad for a local marijuana purveyor. The establishment next door to Stumptown sells THC-infused mojitos now, and cannabis chocolate cake. They've invented new drugs since I got sober and it's weird that I'll never try them. Back in 2006, I stuck with hard liquor, coffee, and cigarettes. I'd never even heard of CBD back then. I just wanted to get fucked up.

Alison didn't hug me when she said hello. She sat down across from me and looked me over, trying to assess what I wanted. I knew that look. Even our shadows leaned away from each other.

"I can't believe you're *married*," I said, keeping my voice light and friendly. I eyed her diamond ring, its edges cruelly brilliant. Fair trade, probably.

"The whole thing happened so fast." She squinted at the sun. "You call in sick?"

"Every sunny day," I said, and she laughed and finally relaxed.

I always used to call in sick when she asked me to. Back in the day, before my drinking got crazy, we spent afternoons in the Rose Garden with our toes in the grass. We counted tourists and ate frozen bananas. I proposed to her as a joke, because gay marriage had just been banned again but I still wanted to marry her. She'd laughed me off; she said, you don't know what marriage is.

Apparently, Stanley had known.

"We're close to your place, aren't we?" Alison asked.

I nodded, tapping a new pack of cigarettes on my knee. "Want a tour?" I shrugged to show I wasn't serious. I knew from the heft of Alison's ring that it would be impossible to get her into my house or coax her into being alone together. Even coffee seemed too much for her, the way she jittered her knees and checked her cell phone.

She rolled her eyes. "Come *on*, Jay."

"You didn't quit, did you?" I asked. "Nobody likes a quitter." The cellophane crumpled in my hand. I offered the pack.

"Well, maybe just one."

I lit mine, then hers; the matchbook almost ripped under the pressure of the match. "Glad you've still got it in you," I said, sitting back in my chair. The sunlight caught the smoke, turned it white and thick. On the wall above us, a blue beagle galloped through an atomic blast of vivid flowers.

"So, tell me about you," Alison said. "What's new?"

"Since the last time we had coffee? That's not a lot of ground to cover."

"A month," Alison pressed. "Come on. Tell me how great things are."

"Not much," I said. I'd casually mentioned Ada on the phone, so Alison didn't think I was fishing. "Still working at the library. Thinking about finishing my degree one of these days."

"Whoa, cowgirl."

I winced. "I know. Nothing ambitious."

My lack of aspirations was one of many things we used to fight about. The more she'd pushed me to grow up, the more I'd resented her. She wanted grown-up things, like a car and a job with benefits, a wedding, a family. All the things that, to me, represented servitude. Why show up every day to a job that makes you miserable? My parents worked their way into debt, buying shit they didn't need—windsurfing gear, a camping trailer, whatever—because they needed time away from the office so badly. Why show up at all, I thought. Just be broke. At least you'll know you chose to be that way.

I got *dirtbag* tattooed really small on my arm as a joke, and Alison punched me right in the bandage. That tattoo never healed right. She wouldn't even touch my arm anymore. She broke up with that part of me, and the rest followed.

No surprise, with my attitude, that she left me for someone like Stanley—a developer from San Francisco with his own condo in the new Pearl District. Probably drove a hybrid. Probably drank a lot of kale smoothies. I didn't know it at the time, but he was part of the new wave of people coming to Portland, gentrifying it. He used words like *genuine* and *aspirational*. Before 2006, I'd never even heard of a lifestyle brand, and suddenly my whole city was being marketed back to me and packaged into some kind of authentic experience. I had so many reasons to hate him and people like him. They came in droves, refugees from the Bay Area, and complained about things like the price of avocados or why we didn't have In & Out Burger.

My favorite bumper sticker says *Go Back To California.*

"How about you?" I asked. "You don't have anything better to do on a sunny day like this? You and the hubs?"

"Don't say that, *hubs*. It's awful." She rolled the cigarette between her fingers. "I don't know why I smoke these."

"Because they make you look sexy."

That made it awkward. Alison dropped the cigarette, and we watched it roll into the crack of the sidewalk, where it smoldered against a bottlecap and a tuft of grass.

"I should go."

"Al, It was a joke."

"I know. It's just—you know." She put her phone in her purse and stood up.

"What?" I jumped out of my chair. I had this crazy feeling that I was going to tackle her and wrestle her to the pavement so she couldn't get away. My ears were ringing.

"I can't talk like that anymore. That's not how we are."

"How are we?"

She put her sandal over the cigarette and scraped her foot in a slow arc over the pavement. "You can walk me to my car."

Her old Volvo station wagon with a dented bumper was around the corner. She still left the windows rolled down. The first time we had sex, it was in this car's backseat, pulled off the side of the road in a state park on the Oregon coast. It'd been pitch-dark; her skin was slick as silk. Afterward, she'd cried and said she was afraid I would take her for granted. She asked if I was a bad person to trust, and it was a relief to tell her no, not this time, I was trying to be good. I kissed her again and again. Everything about us felt miraculous.

For a while, things went really well. And then they didn't.

"I'll see you again soon, okay? I mean it. Pull yourself together." She got in without touching me, slammed her door, turned up the radio, and pulled into traffic. At least she stuck her hand out the window to wave goodbye. The wedding ring was big and obvious as a shining shield.

Feeling like a fool, I slouched the ten blocks home. I sprawled on top of the covers with my clothes still on. I wallowed in that hungover, disappointed feeling. My mouth was bitter—coffee, smoke.

I called her a few hours later and tried to convince her to come out for a beer.

"That's a bit much, Jay."

"I'm sorry, I'm stoned," I lied, and she pretended to understand.

When Ada came home, she felt my forehead and kissed my nose.

"Feeling better yet?" she asked.

"Maybe," I said. And watched as she heated water for tea.

## The First One

Of course I loved Ada. I felt guilty about not loving her more. She invited me to visit over and over, and I said no until she lost her patience and yelled at me and I finally said yes. I came to see her with a huge bouquet of mixed flowers, slightly crushed under my raincoat. After hunting for a vase (Ada didn't have one), we used half a dozen water glasses clustered in the middle of the kitchen table instead.

I promised her to stay over sometime. To myself, I promised to stop lying about where I was and who I was with. I should probably quit kissing other women. Stop collecting phone numbers. Drink less.

I remembered Ada liked daisies best and the fragile daylilies. The flower-stand girl had surrounded them with a spray of fern fronds. I trimmed the stems short and balanced them in the glasses. I kissed Ada's neck.

"Friends again?" I asked. She nodded. "You know I'll come over anytime you want, right?"

"You don't have to."

"I want to," I said. Of course I wanted to. I loved her, didn't I? It was the only thing.

## LOVE AND HAPPINESS

Summer. I borrowed Ted's car and took Ada to one of my old favorite places.

We turned the radio up loud and sang along with the Pixies. It was a Wednesday in June, exactly nine months after we met. Singing was easier than talking. The road absorbed my attention. For a moment I forgot she was with me and let my mind wander. *We will wade in the shine of the ever, in the tides of the summer.*

"Cool." Azure, the sky was, and not a cloud in sight. A crow hopped in the gravel by the ditch. I squeezed Ada's knee. "Did you bring sunscreen? I don't want you to get sunburned."

In the Arboretum, I parked, then dashed around the front of the car to open her door for her. I meant to be better.

"You're already turning pink," I said, smiling.

"Don't make fun. You know I can't help it when I blush."

My lips brushed the prickly flames in her cheeks.

The path we chose wound in and out of sunny spots around trees that wore brass markers. At first, she wanted to read each one—Himalayan White Pine, Grand Fir, Cedar of Lebanon—but she got tired of it and switched to looking for deer tracks.

"How many evergreens are there?" she asked.

"A lot. There's an orchard up the hill too."

Ada sped up so we could walk side by side. "Maybe we should have lunch there or at least sit in the orchard after we're done picking. I'd rather talk to you than just walk single file."

"Aren't you sweet." I put my arm around her shoulders. "We should take turns carrying the backpack."

"There's hardly anything in it."

A mile in, we found blackberry vines growing in a sunlit ditch and giving off a strong smell of baking pies. The cedars were full of cursing jays.

"Jerks," I said. "At least they're not dive-bombing us." I'd come here with Alison two years ago, and we'd found a broken baby bird in the path, its neck crushed. We buried it by the trail at a spot marked by a tall stalk of Queen Anne's Lace. Forest Park was one of the few protected parts of Portland. The Arboretum was a place where only the trees changed. As soon as we were away from the car, off the road, a hush settled around us. The sun peeked through the high hedge of evergreens. We could have been the only two people in the city, the only ones left in the world.

I mean, that's what love is, right? An entire country with exactly the right two people in it.

Ada took a plastic bag from her backpack and started picking, though the biggest berries were out of reach and the ones closer to the ground were already mealy with seeds, spiderwebs, ants. We picked until the sack was so heavy that the ripe berries were crushed to jam-colored pulp. A beetle strutted in the dirt.

In the orchard, we sat under an apple tree. There were others, too: pawpaw, quince, persimmon, and pear, planted in the 1930s. I picked a wrinkled fig out of the grass and chucked it down the hill. In a hundred years, maybe this would be the only part of Portland that would look the same. The fruit would still ripen; raccoons could come and eat it. Ada stuck out her fruit-blackened tongue. Her lips were purple. Her shoulders were dappled with fresh freckles. Overhead, the fat bumblebees spun, harvesting nectar. When she was happy, she looked like Alison.

"You're pretty," I said. I meant to be sincere. I knew, looking at Ada, how sadly grateful she was for the attention, and my honesty, however passing, was enough to blur the sharp edges between us.

Her fingers moved nervously against my cheek.

"What is it?" I asked.

She kissed me. She whispered *I Love You* against my lips, her breath as light as wings. She was always extra sweet when I was being my best self.

I blurted, "We should live together. Live with me."

Ada's mouth opened, showing blue-rimmed teeth. She wanted this *so hard*. I wanted those things too, just not with her, and I didn't understand yet that desire of that kind is not transferable. And you can't lie about it. I was a lot of things then, but not a good or honest person. All I knew was that I had to move forward, but the harder I tried the more tangled up I felt.

"Please," I said.

Ada traced my thumbnail with her finger. "Are you sure?" she asked.

I closed my eyes. The moment slipped by like a silk thread, and I grasped at it. I meant to be true. Buy some extra time. A few more months with Ada and I'd be able to feel the way I wanted to. I'd fooled her so far. I kept performing the act we both wanted so badly to believe.

"I'm sure," I said, trying to keep my voice from cracking.

"Then I'm yours." She smiled, and I pulled her toward me, onto my lap.

Before then, I didn't fully understand why people kiss with their eyes closed.

I meant to make her happy. Hold hands, make promises. Wasn't that what she wanted? More than knowing me, certainly. More than the whole story.

**FINALLY, JULY**

Ada moved in with her crates of magazines and clothes, sorted by color. She brought her collection of mugs from Goodwill, all printed with the names of vacation destinations. Hawaii. Texas. Nashville. Soon, collages covered the walls, the fridge, almost every surface of the apartment. They made the space, somehow, much less *ours* than *hers*. Her stacks of magazines crowded the bedroom. In every corner and against the walls, knee-high stacks of glossies waited to be butchered.

Sweating in a camisole, she sat for hours and carved out letters, legs, skyscrapers—whatever caught her eye. She used a rubber mat and an X-Acto knife and would not be tempted away by anything, not even iced coffee.

I watched her work while I fingered the binding of an old *Vogue*. I had nowhere to sit; her magazines were on the chair, the sofa, even the back of the toilet. "People actually buy this stuff? Crazy."

"They do," Ada said. "That shrine I made, hanging by the bathroom? That's worth at least two hundred bucks."

"That thing? Really?"

She slapped the X-Acto flat against the kitchen table. Sweat glued a brown curl to her forehead, and her cheeks were full and flushed. "Believe it or not, my art is actually *worth something* to some people."

Her cell phone buzzed. She answered it before I could shoot back a response. I didn't mean to hurt her feelings. Too late to apologize. Ada pushed back from the table, went into the other room, and lowered her voice.

I cracked the ice tray over the sink. The fragments immediately melted on my skin. I took a handful of cubes, dropped them into a glass, and waited for the water to run cold. It was supposed to be ninety-five today, but the apartment felt hotter. I heard Ada laugh, then mutter something, then laugh again. I went down the short hall and leaned against the doorway. The ice smelled like the inside of the freezer: stale vegetables, plastic.

"Who is it?" I asked, but she only shook her head.

"I have to go," she said into the phone and clipped it shut. She was still smiling when she turned to me. "That was Arthur."

"You haven't talked to him for ages. What did he want?" The living room was even hotter than the kitchen. The windows were left open, letting in the noise from the street and neighbors. A car honked, and I wondered if it was a secret signal.

"He wanted to hire me for a job. He's doing more house photography and needs an extra pair of hands."

"I bet he does," I sneered. "What does he want your hands for?"

She raised an eyebrow. "We are *friends*," she said slowly. "We were *talking*."

"Just talking?"

146

She went back into the kitchen, leaving her phone stuck under a throw pillow. I heard her voice over the running water. "I thought you'd be happy about it," she said. "You're always telling me to hang out with other people."

I put my glass on the coffee table, where it left a watery ring on the laminate. "I think I'll go out," I called, reaching for my cigarettes and keys.

"Where?"

She was at the table again, hunched over the open pages. Her scraps of paper were everywhere. She didn't look up.

"Out. To smoke." But I knew I could be gone for hours if I wanted. I could come back after the bars closed, when it was quiet and things had cooled down.

As I slid out the door, I glanced at the shrine in its gold-leaf frame. A row of hooked black arms formed unholy rays around a rose-covered blond Madonna. Over her tilted face, a tiny man in a top hat emitted lightning bolts, doves, and typewriter keys. Two hundred dollars, Ada said. Then why was it still in my hallway?

In retrospect, you could say Ada was ahead of her time. She was definitely ahead of mine. The art she made, paper stuff, looked like garbage to me but was actually part of the crafting movement, which ended up being one of the things that put Portland on the cultural map. Her collage was at the intersection of all the things that made my city cool: creative girls, doing things themselves and for each other, by hand, with repurposed materials they'd found and traded. Ada's art was at the cutting edge of that change, which brought adorable, twee shops to North Mississippi and Division streets, places with ampersands in their names and cute genderqueer clerks who knew all about yarn. Ada was the future. I just refused to see it.

**TRYING**

While Ada sweated out July in our tiny kitchen, I oiled my bike chain and found new bars on the other side of town, usually alone. My journal traveled in my back pocket. I was collecting phone numbers again, meeting women, and also trying to write more poetry. None of my efforts worked out, but that didn't stop me from trying. More often than not, I found myself lingering by the payphone, trying to work up the courage to call Alison. I knew the number by heart.

"Hello?"

"It's me," I said. I was at Wimpy's, which was slated for destruction. The real estate on 21st was too valuable to support a dive bar, so it was getting remodeled and turned into a bro bar, where beefy men in embroidered Ed Hardy shirts tried to buy cosmos for women with bleached highlights and sequins on their jeans. Straight people. They really do ruin everything. I had another week before Wimpy's closed and I was going to make the most of it.

The bartender—a California blonde with a horsey face—swirled a bottle of blue liqueur in front of the light bulb. Clots of gnats floated in the syrup. "Are you free?"

She sighed. "Just a minute." I heard a rustle, then a metallic click—a door closing, maybe.

"Still there?"

"Yeah," I breathed. It thrilled me that she didn't need me to identify myself. She knew my voice. The bartender mixed a tall cocktail: candied bugs and tonic water topped with a parasol. She set it by the cash register, cracking jokes with the drinkers at the rack. I pressed the phone against my ear.

"You can't keep calling me," Alison said.

I stared down at that week's pile of free newspapers. On the cover was a thin girl in a bikini and a bear mask jumping on a trampoline. The headline said, *Is Portland's Real Estate Bubble Ready to Burst?*

"We haven't crossed any lines, have we? Just talking about work, our lives. I'm not breaking any rules." I tried to keep my voice steady. The newspaper headline wavered. "I thought you wanted to be friends."

"Jay."

"A friendly drink, that's all. This bar is great." The bartender dropped a lit match into the cocktail. The gnats turned to burning spitballs. The tonic water bubbled as though at a full boil. "You'd like it."

"I'm married, Jay. I can't just—you know, meet you in bars whenever you want. You have a *girlfriend.* Who you *live with.* Quit messing around."

"I know what I want," I said, but the receiver clicked, hummed. I stared at the earpiece, then slammed it—once, twice, too hard—into its cradle.

A decade-plus later, I guess I understand why I kept doing this to myself. There's no unified theory of unhappiness, just alcoholism, and the nature of the illness is that I kept doing the same dumb shit over and over again. I couldn't help it and I didn't want to stop because maybe the next time would be different. I wish Alison had changed her number. I wish I'd gone to treatment. But this was all in the past. And at the end, it was my responsibility to quit killing myself.

But I still had a ways to fall. I was almost twenty-four. I knew enough to figure that I didn't know anything, and that really scared the shit out of me.

## SELF-CARE

I sat on the edge of the bed, staring at my socks while Ada rummaged in the closet for more magazines. I *was* messing around, but Alison liked the attention. I was sure she still liked me. If only I could get her to admit it. Then I might be able to do more than give up on fixing things.

"Are you okay?" Ada asked. "You look sick."

I was actually getting sicker. Every time I drank, I felt as if some deep inherent loneliness was trying to kill me. It got so all I did was drink, pretend, fail at pretending, drink some more. I forced a weak smile. "I'm fine. Getting ready for work. How's your art coming?"

"Arthur, art, Arthur, art," she sang. She didn't notice my mood when hers was so buoyant. She stopped being worried when I was hungover, didn't bring me tea or juice and aspirin in the mornings, and ignored me when I slept over at Ted's. My heart deflated in my chest.

If I hadn't been so low, I would have rushed to get out of there, away from her. I was sick of everything, including this relationship. I was still trying to prove I could move on if I wanted to.

I threw my backpack on and carried my bike down the stairs. Had Alison sensed my secret intentions, gotten scared off? I didn't have a choice, when it came to calling her. My fixation was like alcohol; we both knew I couldn't stay away, had no sufficient reason to stay away. I would do it until I couldn't anymore and even then I wouldn't stop.

I felt no ease until I pedaled up the driveway of the Reed campus. The arching branches dappled the ground with green shadows. Suddenly, I could breathe again. This place never changed, either. A girl walked by in shorts so small I could see a mole on the inside of her thigh, a tiny dot like a constellation, leading me in a better direction.

## Card Catalog

Reed's card catalog was an oak beast. The drawers opened silently. Its joints were worn smooth as vellum. It took up most of the reference room, squeezing the space, nearly pressing against the shelves. I put my hand against its polished flank and touched the brass pull on the LO-LOB drawer. I felt sad in other libraries, where people had to find their books using a computer. Using the catalog was a pleasure, a game. I could jump from subject to subject for an hour. Sometimes, I noted the pathways of my research in my notebook: whales to whale bones to corsets to Victorian women's clothes to Victorian women to Victorian marriage. I kept coming back to the subject of love—or it came back to me, one way or another. One shelf, just eighteen books, was devoted to the study of love as pathology. Thumbing through them, I wondered if the feeling I had for Alison was a sickness.

I had Ada, after all. Alison's doppelgänger. Sweet in her own way, but frustrating too. Something about her made me want to smash a plate, scream, and tear her papers off the walls. The way she sat at the kitchen table with her shoebox of unused clippings, taking up space, infuriated me. I hated the way she waited up for me, no matter how late I stayed out. She *wouldn't* leave home; we argued about it too often.

"Go out, make friends," I would say, my voice packed tight.

"But I live with my best friend. I live with you."

"Call *Arthur*. He'd love to spend time with you. Holding hands. Whatever the fuck you do. Real estate people are parasites."

I'd slam the door, leaving her to cry. But nothing changed.

The girl in the cowboy boots had hair the color of a rubber ducky, and she walked up to me as though she knew I was her destination. I slid open the LO drawer and pretended to pick through the hand-typed cards. Up close, the girl's hair was dark at the roots, dirty black. Her shirt was so thin that I could see the tattoo on her chest, but the letters were too small to read.

"Can I help you?" I asked. She was very pretty: square face, wide eyes. She smiled—*used to getting what she wants.*

"I just came to look up bees." She wiggled her index finger, made a buzzing noise.

I led her to the other side of the card catalog, put my hand on the drawer—first step, catch the thread of her question.

"Why bees?" I asked, skimming the cards with my fingers. I did it quickly, feeling her watch me.

"You're good at that," she said. Her crooked smile. I imagined the transparent shirt in a pile on the floor. Her skirt hitched up, cowboy boots on. My fingers, flickering against her underwear. My cheeks went hot.

"I've worked here for a while."

"Bees are endangered," she said. "Honeybees. They get confused by the frequency of cell phones and wander off from their hives. They starve."

"I didn't know that."

"It must not be in the library, then," she teased. She could have been Alison's twin in that moment. She had that same sureness, funny and serious at the same time. Five years ago. Two years ago. Whenever all those things had happened between us.

"There's always an answer."

"Good. Because I want to know how bees breathe. I've looked around and all the other libraries just have things about beekeeping."

"You don't care about keeping them?"

"Not yet," she said. "Breathing first. The rest later."

I closed the drawer, passed behind her. The IO-IPB drawer whispered open with the sound of paper rubbing on paper. I started to flip through, slowly.

"Your problem is that you're being too specific," I said. I flashed the card in front of her face like a magician's trick. "Here."

"Invertebrates?" she read.

"You may recall that the bee is an invertebrate." That made her giggle. "I'll show you where this stuff is."

I led her far back into a dark room with a single window, framed with honey-colored wood. A sunbeam illuminated a patch of floor. The girl stood in it; her skirt caught the sunlight. I felt along the thick spines of the reference books. The one I wanted was clotted with dust, which I blew away in one puff.

"Found it," I said, and she came to stand at my elbow.

"Finally. I'll *know*," she said.

I knelt and opened the book on the carpet. I was suddenly aware of the great space between myself and the other people in the library, each at their own shelf, bending to read the tiny rows of print. I imagined I could hear them rustling the thin pages far away, like mice hiding under dry leaves.

The girl's knees smelled of saddle soap and grass. Her legs were covered in fine golden hairs. She looked at me over the cliff of her patterned skirt and smiled. We were completely alone. I felt my thighs prickle, as though all the blood in my body had suddenly burst out of my veins.

Ada would never know if I touched the back of this girl's knee. If I kissed my way up her leg. If she shivered like a blade of grass. If she pulled us down to the floor. Whatever happened—it would be a secret.

It wasn't cheating, I told myself. The extra stuff was something I needed, that came to me at the right time. I kept the curled yellow strand

I found clinging to my collar. I taped it into my journal, in the back pages. I washed my face before I went home that afternoon. The suds ran down my neck, releasing a sweet smell that was nothing like flowers.

## BALANCE

At work, I looked for the girl with the cowboy boots—did I even know her name?—but she did not come back. The roses were blooming, and I lingered by the library's open windows, watching the new undergraduates waft among the ginkgo trees. They seemed young, still protected by their parents' money. In another few months, when midterms came, they'd seek refuge in the library with their fingers frantically leafing through the reference books. The place would stink with their stress. But now, summer's last gasp, they lolled like happy dogs on the front lawn, baring their arms to the sun.

I was replacing the battered cards in the catalog with freshly typed entries. It was easy work. I sat in the bay window by the reference desk with my back to the pointed arch leading toward the reading pit, the typewriter balanced on a rickety table so low that my thighs felt the clack of the keys meeting the paper. On my lap, I held a shoebox of creamy cards, blank, the best kind of archival paper.

The librarian at the desk turned to look at me occasionally, but otherwise I was unobserved; my typing made a free-form punctuation in the library's silence. I corrected fourteen cards from the AN-ANN drawer, then slid them into place among their mates. The old ones were kept in a separate box, to avoid confusion. Stained, torn, marked by readers. On the card for *Anna Karenina*, a girl had written in loopy cursive "Free Yourself from the Tyranny of Love!" She'd drawn a key underneath, as though love was a set of shackles that grew on you, link by link by link.

That's how it felt, even though Ada could be so sweet sometimes. She'd been like a little kid lately, excited for school to start. She put away the collages; the magazines went back into the closet. Instead, she baked muffins in the morning and learned to knit. Instead of taking up the whole apartment, she curled up and seemed to need no space at all.

"It's nice to live with you." Our feet touched on the sofa. The television played a sitcom neither of us was watching. Her wooden knitting needles trailed yarn. "Being domestic isn't so bad."

I smiled over my book.

"What's that? More science fiction?"

I showed the cover. "Philip K. Dick. It's the one they based *Blade Runner* on. Very post-apocalyptic." I rolled my eyes. Alison loved sci fi.

Ada nodded but went back to her pattern. "Weren't you an English major?"

"A million years ago," I said. Her forehead wrinkled as her fingers teased out a dropped stitch. "Not exactly the most practical thing to study."

She shrugged. "Those art classes I took weren't exactly practical, either. It just seems like—well, you know."

"What?"

"When was the last time you finished something?" she asked. She lowered her needles to look at me. "School? Job?"

Not bothering to mark the page, I closed the book and put it on the coffee table. Her knitting looked like a meaningless tangle to me. "What are you getting at, Ada?"

"Don't be mad."

"How does anything *you* do have meaning? What is it for?"

She folded her hands. *This is the steeple.* "I'm sorry. I didn't mean to pick a fight." Her voice took on a faint whine. "Please sit down. We were having fun."

I stood up faster than I meant to. "You're right, Ada, this is *so much fun.*"

"Please." Bewildered, her face turned toward me like a flower. Her eyes screwed up. The first stinging tears appeared on her lashes.

I shook my head. When I got like this, my fingers itched. If only she'd apologize—but I was confusing her with Alison again; always asking me to work harder, go back to school. *Apply yourself.* Even now it got my back up. "I do plenty," I said.

"You do, you do," she answered, reaching for me. "I'm sorry."

If this was going to work, I had to be calm. Let her touch me. She stroked the angry veins on the back of my hand. Alison knew how I could be; once, when we fought, I'd run out into the street with my shirt flying open. She used to let me go. I think that secretly we thrived on fighting. *Our* relationship was never domesticated.

I let Ada soothe me and sat reluctantly in my place on the sofa. But I couldn't read the book she handed me. I stared at the shapes of the letters, waiting to feel quiet again.

## CUTTING

I ended up limping in at three in the morning. I'd hit a pothole, blown out my front tire and skidded across the bike lane. My scraped hands fumbled the keys. I rolled the bike into its usual place in the hallway. The bent front tire wobbled in the fork. My palms were studded with angry red marks. The soap would sting my peeling skin something fierce.

"You're drunk," Ada said as I came in. "Again."

"I had an accident," I replied. I was always a bad liar.

I heard crinkling, then the sound of tearing paper. "I have class tomorrow. Today, I mean. I should be in bed." Her voice was high and snappy.

As I walked into the living room, I noticed that the TV was set to the weather channel with the sound off. The cartoon sun frowned, catching a raindrop in his eye. Ada sat on the sofa with her arms folded—a tight, prickly ball.

Beside her was my journal.

The jolt shocked the alcohol out of my body. My stomach dropped into my gut, and my mouth filled with battery acid. Ada glared at me, her eyes dark slits.

"Alison," she said.

The first bead of sweat dribbled into my ear. I wanted to snatch the journal and hide it in my shirt. It looked flimsy as a stamp. The spine was dull from wear. You'd think I would have learned from the last time. You'd think I might have gotten better at hiding my tracks. At the very least, I might have quit thinking my girlfriends were easy to fool.

Her pink lips snarled open. "Anything else I need to know?"

I felt the force of her disgust. I blushed. My vision blurred, the blood traveling through my eyelids pushed against my panicking brain. I hated her for exposing me, for looking so smugly furious, for finding the evidence.

"You spied on me," I said. My voice was low and nasty. She opened her mouth, but I slapped my hands together in the air; the meat sang. "Our lease is up at the end of the month," I said. "I'll crash with Ted until you get your shit moved out."

I went into the bedroom and pulled a few clean shirts out of the dresser. She'd stripped the bedding and thrown the sheets on the floor. The elastic on the fitted sheet puckered into a weak fist.

Ada stood in the doorway.

"You planned this," she said. "You wanted me to read it."

"I need my notebook," I said. I stepped around her and, before she could stop me, I plucked the journal from the cushions. My shaking hands had something familiar to hold, and I gripped the spine as hard as I could to keep myself steady.

"Don't go," she called after me.

I felt a tiny bud of pleasure slamming the door on her voice. Her endless waiting, the clinging—it was as though I'd severed the stem of an ugly flower.

I called Ted from the phone in the lobby. My hand caressed the familiar, scarred black plastic. Already, I had a sense of relief. Escape. In two weeks it could all be over. Ada gone. The apartment quiet. A fresh start.

I left a message, then headed down Belmont to catch the morning's first bus. On the ride across town, I slept in my seat, falling into a sudden dream of scattered birds.

## THE BARTENDER

How much drinking could I do? It was a game. Even when I knelt over the library toilet to vomit whiskey and tater tots, I didn't want to stop. I spent my workday leaning against the re-shelving cart, slowly sliding the books back into their places. The golden card catalog—robust, almost healthy looking—repulsed me. My hands felt dirty, no matter how times I washed them. I wiped my hands compulsively on my jeans. I drove back to Ted's place with my sunglasses sliding down my nose.

"Got your ID?" Ted asked as soon as I came in.

I sprawled on the couch, groaned. "You're going to break me."

"Well," Ted said, pulling off his tie and going into his bedroom. "Dinner first. And I have to change out of my work clothes."

"Therapy is cheaper," I growled. I put my feet on the floor and inspected my sneakers. I had a persistent ache, that's what it was. Nothing seemed to make it go away. Alison still wouldn't answer her phone. I couldn't decide if disappointment was eating me or frustration at saying the wrong thing. My whole plan, if you could even call that, was so stupid and so transparent.

"Did you shower today?" Ted asked

I rubbed my chin. "Sure."

"Go do it again. And fix your hair. We're getting you laid tonight."

I rubbed my eyes. My fingers smelled like cigarettes. My nails were turning a pale shade of yellow.

"You're such a princess, Ted. Costume changes and drinking, that's your answer for everything," I said. He laughed and started singing a show tune from *The Music Man* until, disgusted with his cheerfulness, I slouched into the bathroom. Ted's razor was perched on the slick white sink. I picked it up and twiddled it between my fingers.

"Hurry up," Ted called. "I want to get to Bluehour before the rush."

Bluehour was a nice place, fine dining, New American cuisine. A punk like me would stand out like a sore thumb. The thought made me smile and, instead of slicing my wrists open, I turned the water on and started to scrape the funk off my teeth.

After dinner, we ended up at the Clinton Street Pub on the other side of the river. It was not Ted's usual scene; he stood out here, with his nice jacket and wingtips, but I fit right in. The other drinkers wore dingy black and plaid and left their hair shaggy. They looked like me. The woman tending bar was no exception. Around her forearm curled a mermaid holding an anchor between its breasts.

"She's naked," I stuttered.

The bartender raised an eyebrow. "You noticed."

I tried to regain my footing. Close-up, this girl was pretty; she had a streak of blue in her messy hair. "I noticed you first, though," I said.

She smiled. I smiled back and turned away to the noise of the bar.

"This place is a dump," Ted said. "Below dive, even. The beer is cheap, and somebody keeps playing the same Stooges album over and over."

"Quit being a yuppie. That bartender likes me."

Ted grinned. "I bet you think strippers like you too."

We were squashed at a tiny table next to the pinball machines, which lit up and pinged at odd intervals. The flashing lights were out of sync with the jukebox's ragged bass. I drank my beer and watched the High Life banner over the bar. Its endless ribbons cascaded into a foaming pint glass.

When Ted headed home, I took the open stool at the end of the bar.

"Back for more?" the bartender asked.

"What's your name?"

She shook her head. "Another Pabst?"

"Katie? Christina? Erin? I'm going to guess it eventually."

"Those are white-girl names."

I took the ballpoint from my backpack and helped myself to a stack of flimsy cocktail napkins. The couple seated next to me, wearing matching Dickies and messenger caps, wrapped their arms around one another. Their hands crept under each other's shirts.

"Cool it," the bartender said to the couple. "You guys wanna make out, take it somewhere else. And not the bathroom."

One of them giggled, waved her hand in the air. "Got carried away," she said.

Her girlfriend took her fingers, and they left together. The heavy door sealed in the smoke and noise.

I watched the bartender pour drinks, fetch baskets of deep-fried corn dogs, and coerce the jukebox into giving back somebody's quarters. I wouldn't ordinarily focus so much attention on one girl—usually I waited until they came to me. But I needed a break from my own bullshit tonight. I promised myself: no more bi girls and no more weirdness.

I ordered another beer, this time with a shot. When she came with the glasses, I pushed a new napkin toward her.

*You're pretty.*

She read it, blushed. She folded it in half and slipped it into her shorts.

"You drunk?" she asked.

"Ha!" I tipped back the shot while she watched, wanting her to see me grimace from the cheap, stinging whiskey. She took the shot glass from me. Then she put her tattooed arms on the bar and whispered in my ear. Her breath smelled like cinnamon.

"Brisa."

"I would never have gotten that."

She winked, lifted the Old Crow bottle again. "This one's on the house."

She poured for me, and I passed her notes until closing. *Is it time to go yet?* I wrote. *I want to kiss you.* I paid from a messy handful of ones and fives, too much. I stuffed the change back into my pants, trying to seem only tipsy. At closing time, she shut down the jukebox and pulled the plug on the pinball machines. She switched off the TV, put the key in the cash register, and shooed out the last handful of drunks.

I bent down to pick up my bag. My head felt too full, but her hand was on mine; the mermaid tattoo filled my field of vision.

"You. Wait outside."

I nodded, lit a cigarette. My shadow wavered on the sidewalk. I found that if I looked up, I felt too dizzy and had to lean against a parked car. If

I looked down, my stomach heaved, and my shoes looked too far away. I picked a midpoint on the bar's scabbed wall, covered in torn concert posters and old rusted staples. The wood was ugly, rough in a way that would always reject a coat of fresh paint. I loved everything about it, and I hope it never fucking changed.

"You shouldn't smoke," Brisa said as she locked the door.

I dropped the filter into the gutter. "Look at that. I quit."

"Funny." She crossed her arms, looked me over. "So? What's *your* name?"

"Jamie. Jay," I said. A light in the Clinton Street marquee sputtered, went out.

"Walk me home," she said. She was much smaller than I'd thought. The bar must have a platform behind it. Her body was thick, with gorgeous calves that stretched her leggings to transparency. She stayed in front of me, leading me, and I was sure that she was strutting a little, just to show what she had. The early summer night was still warm enough that she didn't wear a coat. I imagined licking the mermaid's tail, tracing its inky breasts with the pinpoint of my tongue, gripping her hand while she cried out, asked for more.

When we were almost to Hawthorne, she stepped into the doorway of a white apartment building. The handrail was bumpy with moss. My buzz faded. Alcohol didn't work the way it used to with me. Six shots, but an hour later, I'd be clearheaded again, sick, aching for another drink.

"This is it," she said.

I put my hand on her elbow, cupped it. I realized that I was touching a stranger.

"Could I have a glass of water?" I asked. My mouth was suddenly dry as cotton.

Her apartment was on the first floor. We walked past a mirror framed in sterling leaves. A strip of old velvet wallpaper had been left to curl where it hung.

"Glasses in the kitchen," she said, tossing her purse onto the floor. "I'm taking a shower, so help yourself."

When the bathroom door closed, leaving me in the dark hallway, I put my hand on the wall and slowly felt my way toward the light switch. A pile of dishes crusted with spaghetti sauce cluttered the sink. On the counter, there were several mason jars half-full of old iced tea, some still with sprigs of mint and withered lemon slices floating in them like organs in formaldehyde. I shifted the plates aside so I could slip a glass under the running tap.

The water tasted like an old gum wrapper. I shook a few tablets from the bottle of aspirin by the dish soap, hoping to ward off the inevitable hangover. I couldn't remember if tomorrow was a workday, couldn't remember what time Ted said to be home.

"Jay," Brisa said. I turned too quickly to look at her, and my water spilled, splashing the linoleum.

She wore nothing but a pair of small black panties. As I looked at her, she sucked in her belly. Tattoos crisscrossed her legs and shoulders, and even wiggled out of her waistband.

"Still think I'm pretty?" she asked.

When I kissed her, she wrapped her arms around my chest so tightly that I could barely breathe. I felt her tremble—not from excitement, but from an imbalance that made us lurch sideways, then down the hall into her room and onto the rumpled sheets. Up close, I saw that the panties were well-worn; the elastic pilled around her thighs. I traced the polyester lace, and she arched her back. It was as though we were learning to dance, each partner performing the correct movements too stiffly and out of time. Our kisses, even, were dry and polite. *How do you do? Simply marvelous.*

She reached for my belt buckle, popped open my fly buttons. I closed my eyes.

"Wait," I said. "I'm sorry."

She sat up, tucked her knees against her chest. "Is it me?"

"When was the last time you did this?" I touched her hair.

"A while. Jesus." She put her knuckles against her lips. "I'm not going to cry."

I pulled her down to lie close to me. Her leg touched mine—she flinched. I put my arm under her head and lay back looking at the ceiling. She sniffled into my shirt.

"This is so embarrassing," she said. "I thought—you know."

I turned my head and felt her cinnamon breath on my ear. Even in the dark, I could see the pictures on her, and I thought about the hours of pain and the astronomical price of having them drilled into her skin. On her chest, a snake coiled around a cactus; the eagle dropped down from her shoulder with its claws outstretched.

"Mexico," I said, touching the cactus thorns.

"I was born there."

I rubbed the snake's flat head and traced it down her ribcage. Her mermaid swam out of the covers, and I pressed my cheek to it, and her lips found mine;, we were a pair of hot magnets clicking in the dark.

I left in the morning while she still slept, her hair tangled, one arm thrown across her face to block out the sunshine. I considered leaving a note, but the pleasure of walking away for good felt much better. Brisa was someone I didn't have to take care of. I never had to see her again.

I didn't drink for weeks after that. The misery that had been driving me just lifted out of my body. I woke up clearheaded, went to work on time, and quit worrying whether I stank. I felt balanced. Maybe this is what adulthood was like: Instead of doing the same dumb shit over and over and waiting for something to change, you changed yourself and the rest fell into place.

Instead of running around with Ted, I taught myself the basic mechanics of derailleurs, brakes, and cranksets. I tuned up my bike and considered putting on fenders and my seasonal gear. Being out of the bars helped me feel less displaced somehow. I didn't mind new people, because I rarely saw them. I drank a lot of coffee. I slept in on the weekends and never read the newspaper.

"You're boring now," Ted teased. "It's nice. Look at us, a pair of old bachelors."

I nudged him with my toes. "I found a place, by the way. It's close."

Ted squeezed my foot and, although I didn't look up from my book, I knew he was smiling at me. "I love you, dirtbag," he said.

Sober, I had no trouble finding the money for my security deposit. Funny how that works. My new apartment was in a converted warehouse deep in the industrial district. The hall closet was lined in thick lead sheets nailed to the wood by a former tenant.

"I think it was supposed to be a bomb shelter." The landlord swiped a hand over the gray metal.

"On the fourth floor?"

The landlord shrugged. "Don't ask me. Nice view, don't you think?"

On moving day, Ted helped me haul a secondhand futon into the service elevator. We wrestled it down the hall, past the general-use phone bolted to the wall, and into my apartment. We were both grimy, sweating. We dropped the mattress in a corner.

"Does Ada know you're coming over?" he asked.

"I told her. It shouldn't take too long."

He shook his head and handed me his car keys. "Good luck," he said.

I was good, though. I felt like myself. Ada didn't scare me, because she never changed.


## COLLECTION

I could have forced Ada to move out, got part of my deposit from her, or tried to make her take over the lease. But fighting would have prolonged our relationship, which was the last thing I wanted. It was easier to just let the old place go and start over—I hoped with no hard feelings, though I knew that was wishful thinking.

I pulled up to the curb of my old building and set the brake. As I got out of the car, I glanced up. Ada was sitting in our window.

"I came for my stuff," I said. She shook her head. A cigarette appeared in her hand. She lit it and waved at the smoke as though shooing a mosquito.

"On the sidewalk," she said. She pointed down to a row of black garbage bags that crowded the narrow median of grass.

I choked. She'd done it all herself. Probably torn my posters off the walls, crammed them in with my clothes. Who knows what she'd done with the rest.

"I'm coming up," I said.

"No, you're not." She tapped the cigarette, and we both watched the ashes flutter to the pavement. "I did you a favor. Are you hungover?"

"No," I said, and it felt good to tell the truth. *Fuck you*, I thought. All she'd ever done was criticize me. I hadn't had a drink in seventeen days and I felt like a completely new person. She didn't fucking know me.

"Can I have one of those?" I asked. They were *my* cigarettes.

She let the pack fall. I picked it up, shook one out, lit it.

"Where are you going?" she said.

I wasn't going to answer that. The last thing I wanted was to see her again. I shrugged, tried to look like I didn't know. "Not sure yet. You?"

"I'm moving in with Arthur," she said, triumphantly.

I hated her because I knew she'd done it on purpose.

What was it about me that made my girlfriends run off with their male friends? The next one, I promised myself, would be different. I wouldn't have to worry if she missed dating men or if I lacked something that she needed. She would be someone I never wanted to cheat on. She'd be more than just a carbon copy of somebody I used to know.

I sat on the curb next to the bags with my feet in the gutter. A yellow daisy poked through the seams in the concrete, and I counted the petals without touching them. *I deserve this; I don't deserve this.* On any other day, I'd be riding my bike on the waterfront, taking a picnic up to Mount Tabor. Instead, the bags. And not even allowed to go inside, to see if anything was left behind.

What wouldn't fit into the car went into the dumpster. I tossed the bags in, trying not to guess what I was throwing away. I slammed the trunk, leaning hard to pop the latch closed. When I looked up again, the window was closed, and the blinds lowered. It was such a simple ending, so different from what I was used to. Probably better that way.

I muscled the black garbage bags out of Ted's car and through the door of my new place. I had no furniture, not even a table: I'd decided to walk away and let Ada deal with it. I sat on the futon and started unpacking.

Opening the bags, I found that Ada had folded my clothes before stuffing them in. The creases in my shirts pricked my conscience. I could always count on Ada to do something spiteful like that, to remind me that *I* was the bad guy. She'd even taped brown paper sacks over my books to protect them from the move. I wadded the wrapping and threw it onto the floor. *Self-righteous bitch.*

I squeezed my hands into fists. I had nothing and, in that moment, I didn't feel good about it. I had some clothes, my bike, a plain sheet for the bed. A truck went by in the street, and the empty apartment amplified its filthy rumble. This was where I lived now. I punched the mattress, stood up, paced, kicked at nothing. This was bullshit.

I stomped down the hall to the ancient, black rotary phone. I should have called Ted, or maybe even my parents, though I'd quit doing that when I dropped out of school. Instead my fingers, with a will of their own, dialed Alison's number. She answered on the first ring.

"I thought I told you not to call me," she said.

"That was ages ago. Am I off probation yet?" I laughed, but she didn't join in.

"What do you want? I told you that we can't be friends."

"Then why did you answer?"

"Every time you call, it's an emergency. I keep expecting to talk you down off a bridge."

"I'll jump if you don't have coffee with me," I said. "Come on. Please?"

We met at Acorn. One wall was covered in framed doodles of pastel whales, pelicans, and seals. A skinny kid in a plaid shirt pulled a double shot for me and slid the white cup onto its saucer with a flourish. Alison wanted chamomile tea.

"But this is *the* place for espresso," I said as we carried our drinks outside.

She jabbed the plastic ashtray with her finger. "This thing stinks. And please don't smoke around me. My stomach's upset."

I moved it to another table, then watched her swirl the soggy tea bag aimlessly in her glass. The pale-yellow tea was the same shade as her highlights. Her roots were growing in, golden brown. It aggravated me, the way she kept me at arm's length. I just wanted some company, someone to fucking talk to. Was that so much to ask?

"So, what's new?" I tried to get her to open up. "You look healthy. Life is good?"

"It is. Lots of changes."

"How's good old Stanley?"

She pushed her sunglasses up on her head. "Be nice," she said, with the faintest sharpness in her voice. I raised my hands: *Don't shoot.* "Besides, you'd like him if you gave him a chance."

"Sorry, missy. I don't make friends with the competition."

She sighed. "Seriously? Competition?"

Fighting with her made me feel better. I sipped the coffee, winced at the bitterness. "I should have put sugar in this."

"Stanley is not your competition."

"Funny, that's what you said before you dumped me too." Watching the black liquid coat the lip of the cup, I swirled the espresso. "Needs milk."

"I can't believe you," she snapped. "You agree to be platonic, then act like a jealous girlfriend. You invite me to coffee and spend the whole time picking on me. You're impossible. I don't know why I keep thinking this will work."

I sat back in my chair. She was angry now and defensive.

"You're so two-faced," she continued, getting louder. "It drives me crazy. You never knew what you wanted and got mean when I didn't magically know how to make you happy. I don't know why I stayed with you so long."

"Whatever it was, you keep coming back." I smiled, knowing it would infuriate her. She couldn't deny that I'd made her happy, that she'd been attracted to me. No matter what she told her husband, I was proof that she wasn't totally straight. She wanted me then. She might, still.

"This is the last time," she said. She caught my eye, held it.

I tried to joke. "You sure?"

"I'm positive," she said, her voice cold and flat. "After this, I will never see you again. I don't care if you live right next door. We're through."

I laughed, trying to shake off her seriousness. "You say that every time."

"I'm pregnant." She cupped her hands around her tea. "Over the first trimester now. I'm due in early February. We'll know the sex in a couple weeks. You don't have to congratulate us."

That took the wind out of me. *We, us.* It grated on my heart. When she pushed back in her chair, I saw how her belly had grown under her shirt, starting to show. That was Stanley's baby. Alison covered the bump with her hand, guarding it.

"Goodbye," she said. "I don't think I have to tell you—don't call me again."

I watched her cross the street. A produce van passed her, and she waited at the corner for it to turn. My last glimpse of her was of her back as she turned up Glisan and disappeared. She'd walked out of my life before, but knowing this was final made me ache all over.

I staggered back to my apartment as though I was drunk. My eyes blistered with tears. Whether I liked it or not, Alison was out of my system. My throat clenched. I lay on the bed for a long time, waiting for my body to stop shaking.

### FIXED

Fuck yes, I went back to the bar. What else was I supposed to do? Within two days, I was right back where I'd started.

"I've got to stop drinking." I tapped my empty glass. The bartender refilled with a shot of tequila that I knew I'd regret later. But Wimpy's was closing next week, and the horse-faced bartender was playing my favorite Clash album on the stereo, turned up high.

Ted raised his eyebrows at me. "Solve your other problems first."

I grimaced when the liquor hit my tongue and forced myself to swallow it. "This is godawful. You know, I think I'll turn in early tonight."

"What's your rush? My flight isn't until midnight; we've got hours."

"I'm driving *your* car while you're out of town, so I should probably be kind of sober."

Ted shook his head and ordered another beer. "I'm still hoping to come down with something fatal at the last minute. The problem with having so many sisters is that you have to go to their weddings and dance with their ugly friends. Maybe the plane will crash and put me out of my misery."

When his cab came to take him to the airport, I hugged him and said I hoped he caught the bouquet, just to make him laugh. Outside, I lit a cigarette—trying to quit smoking too—and walked around the corner looking for Ted's car. All these blocks looked the same. Big Craftsman houses and apartment buildings crammed next to rows of cherry trees and attractively overgrown gardens.

It was easy to get lost, especially with my mind on other things. I went around the block twice before I found where Ted had parked.

The front end of his car had been smashed. Both headlights were broken. The front fender was bent and mangled. I stood on the sidewalk, my cigarette still fizzling in my fingers. I checked the license plate. It *was* his car. It had my Palahniuk book on the backseat. The driver's side door was scraped; a long ribbon of red paint was missing from the scarred metal. There was no note on the windshield. I couldn't even get the hood open to see how badly the engine was damaged. I imagined, for a moment, that Ada had done it, intentionally wrecked my car just to have some revenge. But she'd need a sledgehammer to do this kind of damage. Someone in a truck had hit it, more likely, and driven away without a second thought.

I walked back to the bar. Ted was gone, but the bartender flashed me a friendly smile.

"Forget something?" she asked.

"My car got totaled. Can I call a tow truck?"

She gaped at me. "Jeez, I'm sorry. Need a phone book?"

She put the yellow pages on the bar and went back to polishing the rows of dusty glasses. I looked at the ads for a long time, trying to make sense of them. I wasn't even sure who would tow at this time of night. The car was too damaged to run, and I couldn't afford to get it repaired. I'd have to call Ted and tell him what happened. He wouldn't be back from Colorado until next week. I didn't even have a number for him, didn't know where he was staying.

"You mind if I take this?" I asked the bartender. Without waiting for her to answer—she didn't even look up—I ripped a page from the book and stuffed it in my back pocket. "Thanks," I called on my way out, and she waved to me through the plate glass window. I didn't linger to see if she noticed my handiwork.

The next morning a fat man with the name Mel embroidered on his shirt hitched the car to his truck.

"You can check with the insurance company, but in my opinion this is gonna be scrap metal," Mel said. He turned on the jack, and the car limped up the metal ramp. "Look at that front axle. You'd never get this thing rolling."

I nodded. Mel handed me the license plates. The car could stay in the tow yard until Ted got home. I couldn't find the registration in the car, no insurance, nothing. For all I knew he didn't bother to keep the payments current.

"Good thing I've got a bike," I said to Mel, who only nodded and hopped into the cab of the truck. Its engine grunted and spat a cloud of diesel-scented smoke into my face. As the car disappeared down the street, I realized that I'd left my journal on the passenger seat. I watched for a minute, then turned away, walking in the other direction. It felt like a good time to get rid of things.

I biked to work every day, even though riding a single-speed made my legs ache. But it was a good feeling. Things were starting to make sense again.

## YOU CAN LEARN A LOT FROM LYDIA

Lydia had long hair that had been dyed many times. At the moment, it was chestnut brown going mousy at the roots. She had a piercing in the center of her lower lip that she sucked on as I talked. A run in her stocking seemed to irritate her, and she stuck her finger into its ladder and scratched her leg. She stared at her empty glass on its coaster. We were the only customers in O'Brien's, the bar jammed next to Wimpy's.

"Do you want another one?" I was back to day drinking. Ted wasn't speaking to me, and I wasn't sure how much I cared. Construction had started next door. Yellow tape stretched across the window. The contractors ripped out the grimy seats and tossed them into the green dumpster on the curb.

"Got any quarters?" Lydia asked.

I extracted a few from my pocket.

"I'm gonna kick your ass at pinball," she said, dismounting her stool. "Watch me."

The only machine was *The Twilight Zone*, featuring the voice of Alfred Hitchcock. Lydia hammered the flipper buttons and tilted the machine back and forth. She got the three-ball bonus and kept them in play for a few minutes before they slipped into the side chutes.

"Your turn," she said, feeding in a few more coins. As I took her place, I read the orange letters on the screen. The high scorer's name was Lloyd. Lydia pulled up a barstool.

"Actually, that's me. It's a joke." She helped herself to one of my cigarettes.

"You're just trying to psych me out."

"It's true. I *am* the high scorer on *Twilight Zone*. You will *never* beat me."

I pressed the start button, making the board light up. A plastic hand reached up from the slot of a tiny grave. "Why Lloyd?"

"Because it's the perfect name for somebody who would master an 80s pinball game. I was either gonna be Lloyd or Snake." She nodded at the ball that was loaded into the springshot. "Don't be shy."

For the first few rounds, I played well. The elevated bridges lit up, and the raven at the top of the board flapped its stiff wings. Lydia leaned closer; I felt her smoky breath on my neck. The ball slipped past me in a heartbeat.

"You probably got screwed on the flippers," she said.

I shrugged, trying to play it off.

"The game was really easy one week, and I guess the company wasn't making enough quarters. So they sent in a repairman with a suitcase full of flippers. They all looked the same, but they were just slightly different lengths. Not so different that you would notice." She nodded to the bartender, who drew two pints. "I watched him put in the shorter ones, and nobody had any luck after that."

"So, it's not my fault?"

"You're no Lloyd," she said. "But you can blame the flippers if you want to." She winked at me over her glass.

On the huge TV screens that framed the bar, a pair of tall blondes batted a tennis ball back and forth. They looked like sisters, tall and corn-fed, in nearly identical whites.

"I'm so bad at sports," she said. "Funny how I keep ending up in sports bars."

I tore a matchbook in half, separating the matches from their cardboard spine. I laid the matches on the bar and arranged them in squares, letters, a house. "I miss Wimpy's."

"Can't keep missing things, though. You'd never stop."

I blinked at her. Ada, Alison. It was on the tip of my tongue to tell her the whole story. Maybe she knew a magic word that would remove my bad luck or a leaf that I could slip into my shoe to lead me to happier days.

"I miss New York," she said. "I miss Chicago. I miss New Orleans."

"I miss the way Portland used to be."

She laughed. "I bet the people who were here before us say the same thing. We're invaders. Even if you were born here, you don't ever really belong." She picked up a few matches, crossed them in an X. "Facts about me: I'm afraid of heights and hissing cockroaches, I've never kissed a guy, and I have dreams about the future."

Ann Peebles came on the stereo, and Lydia sang along, her head tipped to one side. Her skin was fine as milky glass. I watched her lips change shape and imagined how it would be to touch her face—like dipping my hands in a bowl of cool water. When the song was over, Lydia flipped open her phone, checked the time.

"Shit, I gotta go."

"Where?" I didn't want her to leave. We were easy with each other; our words crossed in playful volleys. I liked the way she sang in front of me. She was a chatterbox, but I didn't mind. She didn't hold anything back.

"I promised a friend I'd go to his show at the Goodfoot." She stubbed out her cigarette. Her face settled into a sullen look. "Bad timing."

"Want a date? I'll pay the cover."

"There isn't any cover; he's not that good." She laughed and stuck her phone back in her bag. I saw a cigarette pack in the pocket, still wrapped in cellophane.

"Take me with you anyway," I pressed.

Lydia sucked her lip ring. "You don't *seem* crazy. What's your name, again?"

"Jamie. Or Jay." I spread my arms. "See? Not crazy."

I left a tip on the bar. Outside, she shivered, pulling her jacket close.

"Autumn," she said. "At least it's not raining."

"Wait ten minutes," I said.

"I'm not made of sugar," she said. "Not gonna melt."

On the flat stretches, I rode with no hands, and Lydia copied me effortlessly, laughing when I wobbled. She was almost as tall as me; our bikes were evenly matched. We pedaled fast, even on the hills. It was good to be with someone who could keep up, for once.

When I was twenty-three, everything felt like a parable, a sign. I was grateful for the obviousness of Lydia and the ways she showed me how to find her.

### AGAIN

"You're a bad influence," Lydia told me, bumping her fist against my arm.

I grinned, reached for the pitcher. "You didn't want to see him perform *that* badly," I said. "Admit it. Beer with me is more fun than an open mic."

"You're a very naughty girl," she said, waving her finger at me. She looked past the Night Light's curtains at the steady rain. "Plus, now I have to bike home in this."

I pulled a Connect Four box from a pile of games on the windowsill. "Let's play until it stops."

Two pitchers and five games later, it was still coming down.

Lydia looked up from the score columns. "You look a little green around the gills."

The women's room had two stalls, neither of which locked. I looked at myself in the smoky mirror. My pupils were black pennies. Nausea hit me hard, sent me wheeling toward the stalls. I bent over the toilet, heaving. The beer came out my mouth, my nose. It ran down my chin into the bowl. I felt my throat spasm and tried not to fight it. *You'll be better in a minute*, I told myself. But my guts burned and even when I stopped puking I was afraid to stand up straight again.

I wiped my mouth with a piece of toilet paper, trying not to look at the mess. My hands shook. I pushed the handle, then turned to the sink. Icy water stung my gums. I scrubbed my face with a paper towel, then spat into the basin.

"Do not fuck this up," I muttered to my reflection, nodded, and smoothed my shirt. "Get her number and then go home."

Lydia touched my sleeve when I sat down at our table. "You okay?" she asked.

"I'm calling it a night," I said. "Can I walk you?"

She grinned and stuck another one of my cigarettes behind her ear for later. "I only live around the corner. But don't get any ideas."

"Hadn't even crossed my mind," I said.

I watched my feet as we walked to the door. The soles of my shoes felt slick on the bottom, as though I was skating on a sheet of ice. We went a few blocks, steering over the neat lawns. I realized that Lydia was leaning on my arm for balance. She shifted heavily from foot to foot.

"How drunk are you?" I asked. "Worse than me?"

"Bad influence," she mumbled, grabbing me tighter. She stuck her nose into the sleeve of my jacket. We passed dark houses and cars covered with crumpled canvas. It was nearly midnight, maybe later. My feet hurt. A blister burned on my right heel; I must have worn a hole in my sock.

"Do you know where we're going?" I asked.

"Just a little farther."

A single streetlight cast gray shadows on our faces. The houses were paper silhouettes. Lydia leaned her head on my shoulder, and I sniffed her disheveled hair. Dry and stiff from so many color jobs, it crackled against my cheek.

"You smell nice," I said.

"Because I smell like beer? Man, you've got a problem."

"No, I like your *actual* smell. When I was a kid, we had these big velvet cushions out on the porch. You smell like those, when they'd been in the sun."

"A happy smell." She squeezed closer. I put my arm around her, letting her lead. I liked the feeling of trusting her.

She stopped in front of a white house with a few gnarly rose bushes growing over the rusted shutters. The stoop was covered in old newspapers and pine needles. A cat of indeterminate color sat on a metal chair by the front door and stared at the porch light's dancing moths.

I untangled myself from Lydia. She patted her bicycle's handlebars.

"Bedtime," she said. She touched the buttons on my jacket, then put her hand on my shoulder. "I don't know where you came from," she said.

"I want to see you again." The words were quick to my tongue. My honesty surprised me. I could be like this with her.

"You want my phone number?"

"I want *you*. Not just your number."

She stroked my arm, soothed me. "You want to visit me tomorrow?"

"I'll come back after work. I know the way."

"Bring flowers," she said. "Nobody's ever given me flowers." She tucked my hair behind my ear; her fingers brushed my skin. She was so gentle.

"Anything you want." I leaned forward, inhaling that sweet smell. She smiled, stepped in close. Her mouth was warm and sticky, candy softened in the sunshine. Her body touched mine, and a tiny space warmed between us. When she pulled away, I reached for her, wanting to make her stay.

"I'm glad I met you," she said. "But you shouldn't drink so much."

She slipped through the front door, letting the cat dart in behind her. I watched her through the window. She put her purse on the kitchen table, then turned out the lights. Her movements were slow and simple—the movements of a person who believes herself to be unobserved. With the house dark, the night around me was suddenly chilly.

Riding home, I found my balance easily, pedaling in lazy circles through the interlocking streets. Love, I thought, was no different than riding a bicycle drunk—how the hills melted under my tires, how I never wanted to stop, how, even if I fell, the scraped palms of my hands were singing with light.

## ADA

Although the flower stand only gave a half-hour lunch, Ada had taken an hour and gone to get a haircut at Ward Stroud's down the street. Now, the new style hugged her face in a neat flapper's cap. Her neck, exposed to the cold, felt pink and raw. She pulled her coat collar up. There was a tiny heat lamp in the booth, but she was forbidden to use it—high temperatures shortened the life of the flowers.

She huddled on a stool behind the black buckets of stems, counting the minutes to the end of her shift. Arthur was taking her out. The haircut was a surprise for him, since he'd been hinting that she needed another change. She checked her reflection in the cold-case glass, liking how her face looked heart-shaped. She'd tell Arthur that she was his valentine.

Ada practiced smiling at herself in the glass, trying to look pretty and light. Her face muscles were tight from being pleasant all day. Nobody wanted to buy flowers from an ugly girl, so she dressed fashionably and always wore lipstick. She'd lost weight and didn't need a bra—she was finally thin enough to fit into Arthur's wool trousers. They were becoming one of those neat, androgynous couples who shared clothes and finished each other's sentences. She smoothed the part in her hair. He'd like it.

And then, just before closing time, Jamie walked by. She paused by the lilies. Like everyone else, she looked at the flowers, not noticing Ada. Her messenger bag was new, and she was smiling in spite of the cold. Ada watched her kneel by the buckets and rub a petal between her fingers. When she stood up, she blinked. Ada licked her lips and tasted blood.

"Ada?" Jamie said. Her voice was a whisper.

"It's me. Hi." She was shocked to see Jamie again. All the things Ada imagined saying flitted from her head like a balsa airplane. Her mind went pirouetting toward the river, unable to catch its balance. She had the sensation of falling through the sky into a cold, evergreen embrace. She could hardly breathe.

"How are you?" Jamie pressed her fingers into the wooden shelf in the stand window, as though to steady herself. The skin around her nails turned white.

"Fine." But it felt like a lie. The new haircut, the job, school. She must look so different—a stranger. Living with Arthur had transformed Ada into someone unrecognizable. She wanted to reach for Jamie, to touch her hand, as though that would undo the months of silence and transform them both into who they used to be.

"You look happy," Jamie said, passing her eyes over Ada again.

A lump rose in her throat, and she swallowed hard. Jamie had never brought *her* flowers, and Ada wondered who she was buying them for today. The lost time made it difficult to ask.

Jamie ordered hyacinths and a branch of pussy willow and watched while Ada cut it into twigs. Ada's hands moved unconsciously, twisting the stems into a helix.

"This'll look nice in a vase," Ada said, wrapping brown paper around the bouquet. "If you put them in warm water, they'll release more of their perfume."

"Thank you." Jamie fiddled with the change in her pockets.

"Arthur's meeting me after work," Ada said. "It's our anniversary."

Jamie took the flowers and touched the knot of twine. "You don't have to worry about me, Ada."

"That's not what I meant to say."

"What do I owe you?" She stroked the blue and gray buds. Who were they for?

Ada shrugged. "No charge."

Jamie thanked her politely. And then, before Ada could say another word, she was gone. Ada was sure they wouldn't cross paths again, now that Jamie knew where to find her.

Ada took extra care gathering up the pens and string on the tying bench and wrapping the flowers in plastic. Everything was neatly put away. She tried not to imagine Jamie offering the fragrant bouquet to another girl. After all, *she'd* moved on, hadn't she? They were adults now, just acquaintances. Their lives didn't touch anymore.

Arthur was late picking her up.

"The streetcar was slow," he said as they walked down 23rd.

Ada smiled her used-up smile at him.

He brushed the short hairs back from her face. "You look perfect. A little serious, though."

"Just a long day," she said. She felt a tiny shiver, as though an icy blanket had fallen over her shoulders. "Nothing that can't be fixed."

Arthur took her hand. "Then we'll make you all better again."

**THE ENDING**

Lydia took the flowers. She touched the tiny hyacinth blooms and stroked the pussy willow buds. I couldn't see her face.

"You like them?"

"They look like little bells." She inhaled. "Mmm. Smells like spring."

We were standing on her porch. Soft rain coated the rose bushes, which bore the hard, pale nubs of leaves and budding thorns. A gray tabby with a drooping belly nosed at my pant cuffs.

"You won't believe where I got those," I said.

"Take them out of someone's garden?" Lydia peeked at me over the bouquet and I realized, with an electric jolt, that her eyes were not brown, as I'd assumed, but blue, nearly purple, not quite violet, and speckled with tiny golden sparks. Her lashes were long and very dark, and as she gazed at me my pulse began to pound because I knew, yes, I *knew* that she could see me, she perceived my tiny, hidden soul, and I was drowning in hyacinths, the magic color of her lovely purple eyes. She smiled.

Alison, this is the woman I hoped you were.

Ada, this is who I wanted you to turn out to be.

She is the you I was falling in love with all over again, and maybe it would last this time, since we had both mellowed and were older and had more experience with disappointment. Maybe there's a chance. Maybe I could be sober, this time, if I didn't have to pretend anymore.

"I got them from my ex. We haven't talked in a year, but she was working at the flower stand. I was surprised to see her."

Lydia nodded. "Was it a good surprise?"

"I don't know. She looked happy. But every time," I trailed off. The words roiled inside of me. She twisted one of the catkins off its twig and traced it down her cheek.

"She's not who I thought she was," I finally said.

"People become themselves."

"No, I mean—I thought I was in love with her, but I was really in love with someone else. I kept finding ways to go back."

I shoved my hands in my pockets. My fingers were trembling. She laid the flowers on the metal chair. She took a cigarette, lit it, and balanced it on the porch railing. The rain came down a little harder. It tapped its fingers on the roof. It pinged on the gutter, the roses, and the stiff necks of the crocuses that were trying to push their way out of the earth. The cat took refuge under the chair. Lydia was wearing a white dress covered in tiny blue flowers. A pink silk ribbon was tied on her wrist. Her skin was creamy, eggshell-perfect.

She said, "It sounds like you were trying to say goodbye to each other."

Numb, I nodded and held out my arms. She burrowed her nose against my neck.

"Hello," she whispered. "Hello."

# THE WORLD-FAMOUS CHICKEN TRICK

LAST MONTH, I WAS IN my usual bar and I saw a beautiful woman with incredible hair. Her hair was long and red, with curls that looked soft and touchable, like in a shampoo ad. The bar was not a fancy bar, but I could tell by the way she laughed with her friends that she felt an invisible spotlight on her and that she was *famous*. I couldn't place her, but I knew I'd seen her somewhere.

"Where do I know you from?" I asked. I leaned over their table and they looked up at me, in my ridiculous suit, still wearing my makeup from work. She smiled, but her expression dimmed. "Did we go to school together?"

She was shaking her head, already shrinking. They can do that on command: retract their famousness, like crabs pulling back into their shells. She was ten times more beautiful than her friends. I wanted to touch her hair, take a handful of it, maybe even without my gloves on, and really feel its fineness with my fingers.

"I didn't go to clown school," she said.

Her male friend barked like a seal. "She was in—"

He said the name of a very famous movie, which had a very famous TV spinoff series. I looked at the red-haired woman. Yes, she was in both of those things. That's where I would know her from. Why would I confuse her with a clown? Maybe the hair, and her red, red lipstick. Or maybe it was wishful thinking on my part, because I saw myself as one day deserving what she had.

I don't understand why people *don't* want to be famous. When you're famous, everyone knows where to find you. Your secrets, real and imagined, are juggled like bright balls for everyone to see. When you are extremely famous, you cease to be interesting because everyone already knows everything about you. That's my consolation, I guess: Nobody knows who I am, but I am extremely interesting.

Her smile was fading; its filament was losing light. This was my cue to walk away. I folded my hands over my belly and tapped my shoes. "I wish I had something for you to sign," I said.

Now her lips were closing over her perfect white teeth. She glanced at her female friend.

"Would you like to see my Chicken Trick?" I asked. "It's a crowd-pleaser."

"She's not interested," said the female friend. "Why don't you leave us alone, clown?"

"I'm not a clown right now; I'm off duty," I said, but they didn't laugh. My makeup felt hard against my skin, and flaky. I pulled my rubber chicken out of its secret hiding place. Their eyes widened. Everybody loved this trick. Even grown-ups clapped when I did this one.

"Bartender," the male friend called. "This clown is bothering us."

I started to go through the motions. I waggled the rubber chicken so that it looked alive. Its neck flopped to one side, then the other. My eyes were on the beautiful, famous woman. She was looking down at her lap now, at her folded hands. She was waiting for me to go away. Her friends did not clap when I finished. I made the chicken run back into its hiding place.

"Marjorie, you can't keep bothering the other customers," the bartender said when he had led me out onto the sidewalk.

"But she was famous," I explained. A tear formed by my right eye, and instead of letting it fall I stared down at the toes of my oversized shoes. *I went to school for this,* I thought. *Because I wanted to learn how to make people laugh.*

"How would you like it, if you were famous and strangers came up to you all the time?" he asked gently.

"I will never know the answer to that question," I said.

He sighed.

If I get famous, it will probably be for the wrong reason. That would be a shame. I would like to be famous before I die, if that's an option. I would like to see if I would enjoy it.

I STOOD OUT ON THE sidewalk for a long time, although it was getting dark. I could see my reflection in the plate glass window and I watched myself practicing the Chicken Trick for a long time. When I was satisfied I had it right, I waved with both hands and bowed, as though the whole world had watched it and already couldn't wait to see me do it again.

# ACKNOWLEDGMENTS

THIS BOOK WOULD NOT BE possible without the unrelenting love and faith of my community. Many thanks to my friends, who read draft after draft, came to my readings, and encouraged me to keep going. Lizz Ehrenpreis, Katherine Morgan, Bobby Hilliard, Ryan Hampton, Jessie Glenn, Sire Leo Lamar-Becker, Lori Ubell, Sahar Baharloo and Duncan McRoberts, Claire Dennerlein Manson, and Tess and Brittany Velo—thank you.

Many thanks to the editors who supported my writing, especially the gang at Mason Jar Press, Daniel Jones at *The New York Times*, Michelle Schlinger, and Lilly Dancyger.

Interlude Press brought this quirky collection to fruition through their hard work, dedication, and brilliant insights. Annie Harper, Candysse Miller, C.B. Messer, Zoë Bird, Nicki Harper, Kristin Pape—thank you. I couldn't have asked for a better team.

Much love to the city of Portland, Oregon, whatever you have been and whoever you will be.

And of course, Ivar Anderson, who shared Portland with me, all those years ago.

# ABOUT THE AUTHOR

CLAIRE RUDY FOSTER IS A queer, nonbinary trans single parent in recovery. Their short story collection, *I've Never Done This Before*, was published to warm acclaim in 2016. With four Pushcart Prize nominations, Foster's writing has appeared in *McSweeney's*, *The Rumpus*, and many other journals. Their nonfiction work has reached millions of readers in The *New York Times*, *The Washington Post*, and *Narratively*, among others. Foster lives and writes in Portland, Oregon.

# interlude**press**™

🌐 interludepress.com
🐦 @InterludePress
f interludepress
🛒 store.interludepress.com

# you may also like...

**Olympia Knife** by Alysia Constantine
*Foreword INDIES Book of the Year Finalist*

Olympia Knife is raised by members of a traveling circus when her parents vanish midair during their act. The mysterious fate befalls another, but she falls in love, and, together, the two women resolve to stand the test of time, even as the world around them falls apart. In the tradition of magical realism, *Olympia Knife* is a tale of survival and resistance for LGBTQ folks and all others who live unseen, untethered, or outside the margins.

ISBN (print) 978-1-945053-27-6 | (eBook) 978-1-945053-44-3

**Beulah Land** by Nancy Stewart
*Published by Duet, the Young Adult imprint of Interlude Press*
*Foreword INDIES Book of the Year Honorable Mention*

Courageous teenager Vi Sinclair fights for survival, social justice, and self-defining truth in the forbidding Missouri Ozarks, where, despite her deep-running roots, it's still plenty dangerous to be a girl who likes girls.

ISBN (print) 978-1-945053-45-0 | (eBook) 978-1-945053-46-7